THE ONE WITH THE GUN

He pushed me into the middle of the room and then leaned against the door. There were about ten of them. I fingered the quiet one in the corner as the leader. His eyes were alert and intelligent and he was staring at me.

"Eddie, you're not in a position to make a deal."

"Like hell," I said.

He smiled. We understood each other.

I might have made the door if it hadn't been for the giant grabbing me by the collar and throwing me across the room like a whiffle ball. . . .

"TERRIFYING"
Providence Journal

"SOLID . . . GRIMLY VIVID"
Kirkus Reviews

Other Mysteries by
Stephen Paul Cohen
Coming Soon from Avon Books

ISLAND OF STEEL

STEPHEN PAUL COHEN

AVON BOOKS ◆ NEW YORK

Grateful acknowledgment is made for permission to reprint lyrics from "Motel Matches" by Elvis Costello © 1980 Plangent Visions Music.

AVON BOOKS
A division of
The Hearst Corporation
105 Madison Avenue
New York, New York 10016

First Avon Books Printing: October 1989

FOR MY MOTHER AND FATHER

Chapter 1

It was a dark and forgotten street that had been left to the rats and the dogs, and the junkies. The dreary gray tenements that lined the south side of the block looked inviting compared to the empty shells of abandoned buildings on the north. "Rent Is Torture" was spray-painted across the front of one of the abandoned buildings. In the middle of the street, the rusty remains of an automobile lay upside down rotting and unnoticed, like the desperate bums sleeping on the sidewalk.

I had been down the street a hundred times before and what bothered me most was the rats. I didn't mind the little ones that roamed the cracked sidewalks and broken stairwells. It was the big rats that bothered me, like the one with the mohawk stepping out of the building on the corner of Avenue B.

They called him The Merk. He was big for a rat but small for a human. He stood in the doorway and wiped the sweat from his face with the back of his hand. As I got closer I could make out the part of his head where his left ear should have been, but wasn't. The whole left side of his head was flat and shiny, except near the top, where the mohawk began. He was wearing a sleeveless leather jacket and his arms were full of tattoos. He looked at me and our eyes met.

It was too late to hide so I lowered my eyes and kept them focused on my feet. I walked slowly and counted my steps, while I tried to forget the stories I had heard about The Merk. After fifteen steps I needed a drink more than anything else in the world. After twenty-five steps I was in front of the building and The Merk was gone.

The door was open and the inside of the building was dark. Another person might have gone back to The Pit for a drink, but I had already come this far and I decided to take my chances that Tony had some scotch for me in his room. I stepped inside and immediately felt trapped by the hot rancid air that hung motionless in the lobby. I inched my way along the familiar hallway. Sweat poured from my body like blood from an open wound. I picked up my foot and hit the bottom step on the first try. From there it was easy. I reached the second floor where a splinter of light escaped from Tony's partially open door. A cat crawled in the shadows of the hallway and eyed me suspiciously.

I knocked lightly. It was like knocking on the cover of a coffin. Quiet television voices filtered out from behind the door, but there were no other sounds. With one finger I pushed the door open.

Tony's one-room apartment was the same as always—except for the corpse. A bare light bulb hung from the ceiling over the bed, which sat like an island in a sea of papers, magazines and comic books. A bathtub and a toilet stood in one corner. Tony's guitar with broken strings leaned against the wall in another. The old black and white television sat on a cardboard crate facing the bed. I carefully reached under the crate and pulled out a small bottle of scotch that still had some life to it. They were showing reruns of *The Honeymooners*, and the naked walls of Tony's apartment echoed with Ralph Kramden's voice, oblivious to the puddle of blood collecting on the floor. I took a good long guzzle from the bottle.

Tony still had his shoes on. He was stretched out on the bare mattress of his bed with his eyes and mouth open. His hair was curly and twisted and his face was pale. He was wearing the remains of a T-shirt that was torn and soaked with blood, and the soiled mattress was turning a deep purple. I didn't need a doctor to tell me he was dead.

I put the bottle down on the foot of the bed and pulled off his left shoe. It smelled pretty bad for an empty shoe. I pulled off his right shoe and it too smelled pretty bad, but it wasn't empty. I reached in and pulled out a thick wad of hundred-dollar bills. My eyes were stinging from sweat and I tried to focus them on the money in my hand. Tony had told me that it was five thousand dollars. I couldn't help wondering how much it must have hurt to walk around with a pile like that in his shoe. I pushed the money into my pocket and had another drink.

There was an old bedspread draped across the window as a curtain. I pushed it aside and stuck my head out the window. It was cooler, but not much. The skeleton of an empty building was an arm's reach away and a narrow alley ran between the buildings. It was about ten feet from the window to the ground. It would be easy to jump. Anyone could have jumped it. The Merk could have jumped it.

I was surprised to see Tony in the same dead position when I brought my head back into the room, as if I expected him to be sitting on his bed and twisting his hair around his fingers like he used to do. I took another hit from the bottle. Tony's arms were parallel to his body and palms up so that I could see the multitude of needle holes in his left arm from years of banging up smack. His ankles were chafed and scabbed from wearing cheap imitation leather shoes with no socks and even from where I stood I could smell his feet. Altogether he was an unpleasant sight, and that's not to mention the holes in his chest.

The bottle had about two good drinks left to it. I sat down on the edge of the bed, away from the blood, and drank. Ralph was dressed up as The Man from Space. He was trying to win first prize at a costume party, but he lost to Ed Norton, who showed up wearing the outfit that he wears when he works in the sewers.

Before I knew it I had left the empty bottle on top of the television and I was climbing out the window. I let myself down slowly, holding on to the sill. When my arms were fully extended I let myself drop and landed neatly and quietly in a squatting position. A dog began to bark. I sat motionless as my eyes grew accustomed to the darkness.

After a few seconds the barking stopped and I could see the alley. It was an overgrown jungle of weeds and bushes. I could have used a machete to clear a path out to Avenue B. When I finally got out to the street I turned and walked uptown. I felt myself shiver in the hot city air.

Chapter 2

There was some commotion at the door of The Pit when I got there. Ivan was trying to drag out a young kid who didn't want to go. The kid was grabbing anything and everything: tables, bar stools, people and finally the door itself. Ivan wrestled with him for a few seconds and when that didn't work he punched the kid in the stomach. The kid let go of the door and tumbled out onto the sidewalk. A few of the punks hanging out on the street turned their heads, but nobody got excited. The kid crawled through the crowd to the curb and sat with his head in his hands like he was going to get sick. He'd be lucky if he didn't have a few broken ribs. Ivan stood in the doorway and wiped the sweat from his forehead with his sleeve.

"Shit, Ivan," I said, trying to squeeze past him. "Who taught you to throw around white people like that?"

He grabbed my arm and pinned me against the inside of the door. Ivan the Terrible, as he had come to be known, was not built like an ox, but he was as strong as one. I didn't bother to try to work my way loose. "What's the matter, Ivan, is the heat getting to you?"

"Yeah, it's getting to everybody. You better watch yourself, Eddie, you know what I mean?"

"No. Show me."

He laughed. "Get your ass out of the doorway before I do show you." And he playfully pushed me inside.

The Pit was a long dark bar with a few tables at the back. It was early and still relatively quiet inside: the bar and the tables were full, but nobody was standing. The jukebox was playing "I'm So Bored with the U.S.A." by

5

the Clash. It was a pretty good jukebox and Ivan spent a lot of time trying to keep people from sitting on it. The men's room was chronically out-of-order, so everyone shared the women's room; everyone but the women, that is. They usually walked down the street to use the clean bathrooms in one of the new restaurants with the plate-glass windows and fancy menus.

The bartender, a big Rastafarian named Abraham, was notorious for the three-foot stick he kept behind the bar. Usually he'd just use it to bang on the bar or to poke someone in the stomach, but when things really got out of hand he'd leap over the bar with it and start swinging. He was a good bartender though. He let me drink on credit. He'd keep track of my drinks on a little piece of cardboard we called my scorecard. Lots of times he'd pour me a drink and forget to mark it down. There was nothing special about The Pit, but it was more fun than drinking at home and cheaper than drinking at the clubs.

I went to the telephone in the back and called the police. A woman with a husky voice answered and I told her where she could find a dead body if she was interested. She thanked me and then asked me for my name, address and telephone number. I told her I was The Man from Space and hung up. Then I pulled up a stool next to Leon at the bar and Abraham poured us drinks. I told Leon how I'd found Tony and about The Merk, and we talked about Tony.

We'd both met Tony about four years ago when his band, Dementia, was playing the East Village clubs. There were a lot of us hanging out in the clubs in those days. No matter what club or bar I walked into, it seemed as if I knew everybody. It was a never-ending party that just drifted from club to club.

I first saw Tony at CBGB's in 1979. Dementia had just been written up in *The Village Voice* and there was real excitement in the air, as there always was when a new band was breaking out. Between bands I stepped outside for some air. It was one of those late nights in the early fall when the first nip of cold air blows through the streets and the next day only those who were awake and out would know about it. We met outside and just started talking and laughing. I don't know what we were talking about, but when I met him again a few weeks later at Berlin, an after-hours club, it was like running into an old friend. Pretty soon we were hanging out together.

At that time he had a girl friend named Gloria, a blond bombshell from Chicago, or someplace like that. She dropped out of the picture at about the same time Tony started getting heavily into drugs. Everybody from the old days was getting into something then. Some got into drugs. Some got into law school. Leon and I got into booze.

Abraham came over and poured us another drink.

"Hey, Abraham," I said. "What's my scorecard look like?"

"Same as always, only worse. Man, one of these days you got to get yourself a job."

"Yeah? Well, what do I owe?"

He reached behind the register and pulled out the score-card. "Eighty-eight bucks, man."

I pulled one of the hundred-dollar bills out from my pocket and slapped it on the bar. "Call it even." Abraham and Leon stared quietly at the bill.

Suddenly Leon began to laugh. "Jesus Christ, Eddie! What'd you do, win the lottery?"

"No, my old man sent me some dough, that's all."

Abraham picked up the bill and looked at it carefully, as if he'd know a counterfeit bill if he saw one. "I don't believe this shit. This be the first time you don't owe me money since the day you stumbled in here."

"Well, how about some free drinks?"

"Yeah, you got it."

Leon couldn't hold his excitement in any longer. "Yahoooo!"

I grabbed my free drink and leaned my back against the bar to face the growing crowd. They were the same familiar faces of East Village derelicts. Punks with broken teeth and scars. Girls with leather jackets and chains and wild makeup. Old men who would be found sleeping in the corner at the end of the night. Students down from uptown for some fun and adventure. Dungaree jackets with buttons that said things like "Who needs life, I get high on drugs." Hair that had been teased, dyed, frizzed, braided, chopped off, mohawked, dreadlocked or just plain forgotten about. There was only one thing that all these people had in common. They were ugly. This wasn't a bar for the beautiful people. It was an ugly person's bar.

A girl with a safety pin in her ear and feathers in her hair came up to us. She was bombed out of her mind, and she spoke slowly and deliberately. "I want to have a drink with you guys." She leaned against me and I felt her feathers tickling my chin. I casually pushed her off me and Leon slipped his arm around her. I wasn't in the mood for strangers.

Leon and the girl started laughing hysterically about something, but Leon suddenly got serious and leaned toward me. "Hey, Eddie. You think The Merk did it?"

"What do you think?"

"I think he did it, Eddie. That guy's a fucking maniac. His left ear is missing. That's some weird shit. Ask Abraham about The Merk. Abe says that The Merk is the only fucker in the world that Ivan is scared of. Can you believe that? Fucking Ivan?"

"What happened to his ear?" asked the girl, still leaning on Leon for support.

"Can you believe that?"

"Did Tony get his drugs from The Merk?"

"Who knows? But I'll tell you something." He leaned over conspiratorially, knocking over a glass in the process. "People say that The Merk runs the show over on Avenue B."

"What happened to his ear? Hey, which one of you guys is going to buy me a drink?"

"Runs the show?"

"The drugs, man. The Merk is the boss of all of it."

"Really?"

Leon shrugged. He was too far gone to appreciate the difference between fact and fiction. Besides, the girl with the feathers was sticking her hand in his shirt.

"C'mon, buy me a drink."

He looked at me. "Should I buy her a drink?"

"It looks like she wants one. Go ahead, buy her a drink. I won't tell anyone she's under age."

"I'm not under age. You can ask Ivan."

"Like I said, buy her a drink."

She hooked one of her fingers into a belt loop on my pants. "I like you. I want to drink with you too."

Leon finished what was left in his glass. "I'll tell you what we'll do. You want to drink with both of us, right? You have one drink for each drink that each of us have. How's that sound?"

"You buying?"

"No, Eddie here's buying."

Leon looked at me over her shoulder and raised his eyebrows. I smiled, but I suddenly felt very depressed.

Abraham came by and poured us another round of free drinks. I took mine and listened to Leon and the girl joking around. Something was very wrong. I stood staring at the graffiti on the far wall above the heads of the East Village unusuals and, on the third drink, it came to me. Tony was dead, and I was drunk. I didn't know what it was, but there was something very wrong about that.

I finished another drink and then started to leave, but Leon caught my arm. "Hey, where you going?" The girl had both arms around his waist and was trying to kiss his neck. His eyes said, "Don't leave me alone with her."

"I got to get out of here."

"What's the matter?"

"I'll be all right. I just need to get some air."

Outside, Avenue A was a zoo. It was another hot and restless Friday night in the East Village. The weather reports had said that it was going to start getting cooler, but I didn't believe it. I didn't believe it would ever get cooler. We were all just going to get fried in the city streets. It was the end of an era.

I made myself comfortable on the hood of an old Chevrolet parked out in front of The Pit and watched the parade of punks swarm up and down the street. Tony was dead and I was drunk. So what? Was I supposed to stay sober because he was dead? Would he have given up smack if he found me dead? Why was it that I found him dead instead of him finding me? It could have been either way. I was never very good at math, but it seemed to me there was a fifty-fifty chance that it could have been either way. But I found him. The odds were even and I just got lucky. And goddamned depressed.

Tony was never depressed. At least not until toward the end. Maybe he knew that it was going to happen. That might explain a few things. The way he talked about everything in the past tense. And the five thousand dollars that he told me he had in his shoes, but never told me where it came from. He talked about himself more in the last two weeks than he ever had before. That seemed strange to me now. I'd known Tony for four years and yet only last week had I learned that he had family out in New Jersey. His brother owned a nightclub in Hoboken called Sanka's. That was the weird thing about New York. You made a friend, you hung out together, got high together, went to see movies together, and then after four years you find out that the guy has family out in New Jersey.

Four years. Now he was dead, and I was dead drunk. Was it possible I had known him for four years? What had I done in four years? What did I have to prove that I had even existed for four years? I had nothing but a good line of credit at The Pit. And $4,900 in my pocket.

I suddenly realized that I had been staring at The Merk for the past ten minutes. He was sitting on the wall of Tompkins Park right at the corner of Avenue A and Seventh Street with a group of punks. They were smoking cigarettes and making lots of noise. The crowd that hung out on that corner was distinctly nastier than the punks on the rest of the block. They were the hard-core motorcycle punks. Leon once said that they were into the violence of punk, not the art of it. I never paid much attention to them. I guess I knew that The Merk was part of that gang, but now seeing him there with them was like seeing the town bully at home with his family.

The Merk was smaller than most of them. The guy sitting next to him looked like he could pick up a Harley Davidson with one hand. His feet hung a full foot lower down toward the sidewalk than The Merk's. The one standing in front of The Merk had a spiked mohawk and tattoos on the bald parts of his head. There were a few girls with them too, or I guessed they were girls. They had no hair, but they had on jewelry and makeup.

The Merk got up and stamped out his cigarette. Then he slapped five with a few of the guys and turned the corner down Seventh Street. Instinctively, I jumped off the Chevrolet and followed him. He was walking toward Avenue B on the park side of the street, so I crossed over and walked on the other side about a hundred feet behind him. There were enough people around so that I wasn't afraid of being noticed. But when I got past the Red Rockets Lounge, the crowd thinned out a little bit, and I had to walk close to the buildings to stay in the shadows.

He had a peculiar walk. At the end of each step he'd lift himself up on his toes before picking up his foot, so that the top of his head sort of bounced up and down with each step. Maybe it was his way of making himself look taller. About halfway down the block he stopped and turned around, to put his back to the wind to light a cigarette. I ducked into a doorway. He would have seen me if he'd been looking for me, but he just turned around again and continued bouncing toward Avenue B. When he got to the corner he looked up and down the street but didn't cross. Then he leaned against a parked car and blew smoke rings.

I watched him for about ten minutes. There were few cars on Avenue B. An occasional taxi went by. He finished his cigarette and lit another one. Finally, a big black limousine with tinted windows pulled up in front of him. He got in the backseat and it took off.

I guess The Merk was doing something right if he could get picked up by a limousine. Even if it was killing poor helpless junkies.

Chapter 3

I lived in a loft down on Christie Street, a block from where the whores worked. Holly was the only one I liked and she was out there, walking up and down the sidewalk, wearing her tight cutoff shorts with the sequined top that made her breasts look big. This wasn't the high-rent district for prostitutes. I had grown to hate the way Holly dressed. Maybe it was because I knew her, or maybe because she was older than the other girls on the block, but she always looked like a woman pretending to be a hooker.

She smiled when she saw me and stepped back into the shadows to take herself off the market. "Hi, Eddie!"

"Hi, Holly. What's going on?"

She shrugged and crinkled her nose. It was a gesture of hers that I had never figured out. Sometimes it was flirtatious. Sometimes she did it when she didn't like something. And sometimes she did it just because she didn't have anything to say.

"Wanna come up?" I asked.

"I can't, Eddie, it's Friday." She pulled a hairpin out from the back of her head, and her dark curly hair fell down on her shoulders. "I could make a hundred if I work the night." She put the pin in her mouth while she pulled her hair back with both hands, then she held her hair with one hand and took the pin with the other and repinned it.

I pulled a hundred out of my pocket and held it out for her. She finished with her hair and took it. "Eddie, where'd you get this?"

"I found it. Let's go."

She grabbed my neck and kissed my cheek. Then we

held hands and walked to my building. We didn't say much. Things with Holly were always a little bit awkward until we were in my apartment. In the apartment we were friends, but out on the street we were just a john and a hooker. The elevator was still broken and we had to climb seven flights of stairs. When we got to the fourth floor, Holly stopped and leaned her hand on my shoulder while she took off her spiked high heels. We held each other and I gave her a trial kiss. It felt nice, but not great. We hadn't made the full transition yet.

When we got upstairs I put on the radio and poured us each a scotch. Holly changed into one of my T-shirts and made herself comfortable on the bed, where the breeze from the fan was the strongest. I handed her her drink and took mine to the window and stared out at the Brooklyn Bridge.

"Is this Elvis Costello?" she asked

"No, it's Johnnie Walker Red."

"No, really."

"Yeah, it's Elvis Costello."

"You like him a lot, don't you?"

"Yeah."

I sat down in the big armchair, facing her on the bed. With her high cheekbones, full lips and dark complexion she could have been Italian or Greek, but she wasn't. She was Polish. It was funny how we had grown to be friends. I had noticed her working the block. We'd say hello to each other, but she never tried to solicit me. Then one night I was drunk and desperate, and I picked her up. We went up to my apartment and started drinking and talking. We got so bombed that neither of us could do anything and we fell asleep on the floor with all of our clothes on. When I woke up the next afternoon, there was a pillow under my head and a blanket over me and a little note that just said "Thanks." I still paid her for her time, but she usually gave me a break. A really good break. We had never seen each other when she wasn't working. She told me that she lived down on Delancey Street. I didn't know. Maybe she had family out in New Jersey too.

She took a long sip from her drink. "You know what one of the girls told me tonight?"

"What?"

"She said that they were going to build a low-income housing project on our block."

"Which block?"

"Down the street, where I work. You know that big empty parking lot? Right there."

"When'll it happen?"

"I don't know."

"How's the jewelry business?"

She laughed. "You want to know the truth?"

"Yeah, the truth."

"I haven't worked on it in months."

"What about the catalog you were putting together?"

"It's still there. I have about fifty pieces designed and ready to go. But I just can't get it together to get them photographed. I don't know, Eddie, let's talk about something else."

"Is it money?"

"Is what money?"

"Is the reason you haven't worked on it money?"

"No, not really. I'm just lazy. Well, maybe it is money. I mean if I didn't have to work I'd have the time and the energy to work on the jewelry, you know what I mean?"

"How far would five thousand dollars get you?"

She laughed. "I'd sleep with you for a year. Hell, I'd even marry you for five thousand dollars."

"No, I mean how far would it get you in the jewelry business?"

"Oh Christ, I don't know. I told you, I don't want to talk about it." She got up off the bed and took the empty glass out of my hand and repoured us drinks. I took my glass and rotated it against my forehead to cool off. Elvis Costello was singing:

Falling for you without a second look,
Falling out of your open pocketbook,
Giving you away like motel matches,
Giving you away like motel matches.

Holly sat on the arm of the chair and put her arm around me. "What's the matter, Eddie?"

"I want to invest in your jewelry business."

"That's sweet. What are you going to invest?"

I stood up and pulled the pile of hundreds out of my pocket and threw them down on the coffee table. "I haven't counted it, but it's about five thousand dollars. You can leave me a hundred if you want to, but the rest is yours. And when your business takes off you can . . ."

"Eddie! Where'd you get this?"

"I found it."

"C'mon, Eddie, where'd you get it?"

"A friend left it to me. Look, don't ask questions. Just take it."

"I won't take it unless you tell me where you got it."

And suddenly I was telling her, but I was telling her all wrong. Instead of telling her about the money and The Merk and jumping out the window, I was telling her about the smelly hall and the blood and the guts. I told her about the puddle on the floor and about how I sat there and drank scotch and watched the television. I told her that Tony was dead and that I wasn't sure if I ever really knew him. I told her that I was a no-good drunk.

I talked hard and fast, and when I was finished I was out of breath and I was shaking. I got up and poured myself another drink and sat down on the bed and stared at the ceiling.

When I looked down she was standing at the foot of the bed and smiling.

"What are you smiling at?"

"You."

"What about me?"

"You used to say you weren't an alcoholic, just a heavy drinker." She sat down next to me on the bed and put her hand on my leg. "Eddie, what's bothering you?"

"Leave me alone."

She lay down next to me and put her arms around me. I was too confused to respond, but it felt good. She was just a whore who worked on my block. I slept with her sometimes. Sometimes once a week. Sometimes not for a month. But right now she was the only friend I had.

"Holly, I'm scared."

I felt her arms pull tighter around me, but she didn't say anything.

"I don't want to get shot to death in some hole. When I die I don't want some asshole like me coming in and taking my money and finishing my scotch."

Holly sat up and faced me. "You really want me to take this money?"

"Yeah."

"Will you promise me something?"

"What?"

"Promise me you'll quit drinking?"

"What?" In defiance I tried to get up to pour another, but she held me down.

"You can do it."

"Yeah, but I don't want to."

"Yes, you do."

"I do not!"

"Eddie, listen to me. I got my uncle to quit drinking once. You know how I did it?"

"Is this a joke?"

"I took away his booze one morning and gave him a tape recorder with a microphone and told him just to say the word 'booze' every time he wanted a drink. He went and checked himself in with AA that afternoon."

"Yeah, well, your uncle sounds like a hell of a guy."

"I'm serious!"

"Holly, take the money and get out of here."

She put her head down on my chest. "Eddie?"

"What?"

"I'm sorry about your friend Tony."

"Yeah, me too."

"I'll take the money, Eddie, but I'm not gonna leave yet. And I'll tell you something, and you don't have to believe me or answer right now, but I just want to say it."

"What?"

"I'm only taking the money because I know if I do that you'll quit drinking."

"And how do you know that?"

"Because I know you, Eddie."

Chapter 4

"Booze."

Somebody might have whispered it in my ear. "Booze, booze, booze." It sounded like my voice. "Booze, booze, booze, booze, booze." It was my voice. "Booze! Booze! Boooooooze!"

I sat up and opened my eyes. Holly was gone. The money was gone. My head hurt and I was nauseated and sweating. I said "booze" a few times softly just to calm myself down. Then I got up to get a drink.

A little piece of paper was taped to the bottle. It said "Booze." I crumpled it up and threw it across the room. I got out a shot glass and poured myself a shot.

A shot of scotch is just brown liquid in a little glass. It's no big deal. I liked to have a few in the morning. Some people drank orange juice. Scotch was just like orange juice, at least until it hit the back of your throat. Then it burned like kerosene and ricocheted around your chest, sending shivers down your spine. Slowly it seeped into your blood and warmed your feet and your fingers. The first shot was the best. But this morning I just sat and stared at it.

I don't know what made me turn and look at my stereo, but I wasn't surprised to see that the microphone had been plugged into the tape deck. I exchanged a few glances with the microphone and the shot of scotch, my eyes finally coming to rest on the microphone.

OK. I'd show her.

I pressed the record button on the tape deck and sat down on the edge of my bed with the microphone in my sweaty hand. "Booze." That was easy. "Booze, booze, booze, booze, booze. OK? Booze." I took a few deep breaths. "Booze." No problem. I was just going to sit there and say the word "booze" for a while. "Booze." It would be like a mantra. "Booze, booze, booze, booze, booze, booze." So what? I might as well have been saying "orange juice." "Booze. Lots of booze. Gallons of booze. An ocean liner filled with booze." My foot started tapping. "Booze! Booze! Booze!" I wiped the sweat from my face with the sheet. "Boooooze!"

"Booooooooooze!" I was screaming. "Boooooooooooze! Goddamned fucking pain-in-the-ass booooooooooze!" I kicked the little table and the shot glass on it went spinning across the room. "Booooooooooze." I threw the microphone at the tape deck and let out another one. "Boooooooooooze!"

I stood there sweating. Then I realized that someone was knocking at the door. "Booze," I heard myself say. The knocking continued. A muffled voice said, "Mr. Margolis, are you in there?"

"Booze."

I put on a pair of pants and a shirt, and opened the door. Two men stood there, panting and sweating. "What's all the screaming about?" the bigger one asked as he squeezed past me.

The other one stayed in the hall. He was a little bit younger and evidently still felt it necessary to flash his badge and identify himself. "I'm Deputy Commissioner Sidney Philips of the New York Police." I looked at his badge and that's what it said, but he looked more like a politician than a cop. He wore a clean, pressed navy blue suit, with a white shirt and a bright yellow tie. Stiff clean cuffs with big golden cuff links stuck out from under his suit jacket and his neat small hands looked as if they had been manicured. Everything would have been perfect except that he was drenched with sweat. Even so, all I could smell was cologne. He had a baby face with big bushy eyebrows that looked like they belonged to someone else. It gave him a sort of comical appearance. "That's Detective Charles Murphy from the narcotics division. Your elevator is broken.''

"I know.''

From behind me I heard Detective Murphy say, "We just walked up seven goddamned flights of stairs.''

"If I'd known you were coming I would have moved down to the first floor.''

Philips followed me in and I shut the door. Detective Murphy picked up the shot glass, miraculously unbroken, and held it in the air to inspect it.

He was bigger than Philips, and he looked a lot more like a cop is supposed to look. He had a big square face with a little bit of fat on his cheeks. With his graying hair and receding hairline, I figured he was about fifty. He also had an annoying smirk on his face, like he knew something that I didn't. Maybe he did.

"You're Edward Margolis, The Man from Space, right?''

"I'm Eddie Margolis.''

"What are you, Greek or something?''

"My father's Jewish.''

"You look Greek.''

"My mother was Cuban.''

"Jesus Christ, a Cuban Jew. I swear I've seen everything. How come you didn't tell us who you were last night?''

"What do you mean?''

Then Murphy spotted the microphone still swinging from the tape deck. He stopped the tape and hit the rewind button. Then he hit the play button. ". . . of booze. Gallons of booze. An ocean liner filled with booze.'' We listened to the whole thing. Murphy was chuckling. He was getting a kick out of me and he wanted me to know it. When it was over he sat down in the armchair and put his arms behind his head. "What the hell is going on in here, Margolis?''

"What's it to you?''

"Did we catch you on a bad morning?''

"Every morning is a bad morning,'' I admitted, and I flopped down on the bed to take advantage of the fan.

Philips stood by the door, biting his thumbnail and watching me. Murphy's eyes moved slowly and carefully around the room. That was all right. I had nothing to hide.

"What do you do, Margolis?" asked Murphy, looking down around the edges of the bed.

"I'm unemployed."

"Well, what do you do when you work?"

"Either quit or get fired."

He laughed. "Where do you get your money from?"

"I borrow it."

"Who would lend you money?"

"Some people are stupid."

"Got any money now?"

I shrugged. "No."

"None?"

"What's it to you?"

"Well, what the hell is this?" He leaned forward and picked something up from the floor by the foot of the bed. It was a hundred-dollar bill. "Where'd this come from?"

"My father sent it to me."

"Your father?"

"Yeah, my father."

"Is he unemployed too?"

"No, he's retired."

"From what?"

"He was a customs agent down in Florida."

"Oh!" Murphy threw the bill down on the coffee table and put his hands back behind his head. "Son of a cop."

"So what?"

"Does he know you're unemployed?"

"Yeah."

"Does he know you're a drunk?"

"Look. What do you guys want anyway?"

"Does your father know you're a drunk?"

In less than a minute this goddamned cop had found my weak spot and he knew it. He didn't even have to say anything. He just sat there with that smirk on his face.

My father and I were friends more than anything else. We went fishing together and we laughed a lot. He never put any pressure on me. The problem was he was so successful at everything he did. He didn't leave any room for me to do anything. Maybe that was why I had left Homestead. My father didn't care if I was a drunk. What I did was my business. And yet I couldn't think about him without feeling like a failure.

Murphy nodded to Philips and said, "Go ahead, Sid."

Philips stood leaning against the door as if he were afraid to come in. "Mr. Margolis, you don't have to make this hard on yourself. OK? We know a lot more about all this than you think. Last night you reported that you had found the body of Anthony Santucci in his apartment. Why didn't you tell us who you were?"

"I don't know what you're talking about."

"Oh come on, Margolis!" Murphy exploded. "Don't give us that shit! We're not fucking stupid, you know. Santucci's dead. We find out who his friends are, where they hang out, and we ask a few questions."

Philips shook his head at Murphy, cutting him off. He could handle me. "OK, Mr. Margolis. How come you didn't leave your name and number?"

"I didn't think you'd care."

"Bullshit!" Murphy screamed.

Again, Philips cut him off, this time by holding up his hand.

"Did you actually see the body, Mr. Margolis?"

"Yeah, I saw it."

"So you had been in Mr. Santucci's apartment."

"So what?"

"So you were at the scene of the crime either during or shortly after the murder."

"Who said anything about murder?"

Murphy chuckled. A real cop would enjoy that line coming from a suspect.

"It would be a most unlikely suicide, Mr. Margolis," Philips answered seriously. "When exactly were you in Mr. Santucci's apartment?"

I shrugged. "I don't know."

"Ten?"

"No, later than that."

"Midnight?"

"Maybe. Maybe earlier."

"You're not being very helpful."

"Buy me a watch and the next time I find a corpse I'll make an exact note of the time."

"What was your relationship with Santucci?"

"We were friends."

"You knew him well?"

I thought about his family in New Jersey. "No."

"The truth is that you went there to sell him drugs."

"No."

"Well, then why did you go there?"

"To sell him Girl Scout cookies."

Murphy chuckled but didn't say anything.

Philips continued. "Don't get smart, Margolis. I'll ask you again. Why did you go to Mr. Santucci's apartment?"

"To visit."

"To visit?"

"That's right."

"What do you mean, to visit?"

"To stop by. To say hello."

"You mean it was social?"

"You're catching on."

"Was he expecting you?"

"I don't know."

"Well, did you tell him you were coming?"

"I don't think so."

"What happened when you got there?"

"Nothing happened. He was dead."

"What'd you do?"

"I left."

"You walked in, you saw him and you left. Right?"

"So what?"

"Where'd you go?"

"To The Pit. It's a bar on . . ."

"I know where it is. That's where you called us from. What'd you do after that?"

"I had a few drinks and went home."

"How come you didn't tell us who you were when you called us?"

"I was hoping I could avoid all of these stupid fucking questions."

I watched his face get red, and I watched Murphy enjoy every second of it. Murphy probably would have grabbed me by the throat and thrown me against the wall. Philips just got red and held it all in. Then he walked closer to me and stood a few feet away from the bed. He was calm, but not as calm as he wanted to be. "Mr. Margolis. You're fucking around with the wrong guy. OK? Now let me tell you what you've told me so far, and you tell me if it's right. OK? You and Santucci were friends. You say you didn't know him well, but you went to pay him an unexpected social call around midnight. You got there and your friend was dead. You walked out, went to The Pit and called the cops without leaving your name. You had a few drinks and then went home. Is that right?"

"So what's the big fucking deal?"

Murphy couldn't take it anymore and he broke in. "The big fucking deal, Margolis, is that right now you are our prime suspect. Now if you want to stick to this ridiculous story, that's fine. We'll drag you down to the station and make sure you get it right. Or, if you feel like cooperating with us, we can talk here and now, like gentlemen. Now, tell us the truth, you went there to sell him drugs, didn't you?"

"No."

"And you went by yourself or with somebody else?"

"By myself."

"Your friend waited outside?"

"No. I went by myself."

"Or did you wait outside while your friend went in?"

"I told you. I went by myself."

"It would be a shame to take the rap if somebody else did it."

"I'm not going to take the rap! I didn't do it! I was the one who called you guys in the first place, remember?"

"That doesn't mean shit, Margolis. You didn't leave us your name. You're up shit creek."

I got up to get the scotch. I was going to need that drink after all. Murphy saw me going for the bottle and he snatched it away from me.

"Hey! Gimme that!"

"Not until you start giving us some good answers. You've given us nothing but shit. Now give me something I can sink my teeth into and I'll give you your bottle."

"OK. I'll talk. Just give me the bottle."

"Nope. Talk first. Then you get the bottle."

"No deal." I went to grab it out of his hand, but he threw it to Philips. Then I went to grab it from Philips, but he threw it back to Murphy. I started again for Murphy, but Philips grabbed my arm and twisted it behind my back.

Murphy was laughing. "You kill me, Margolis. You know that? You really kill me."

Philips let go of my arm and I sat back down on the bed in defeat. I was sweating again. "What do you want from me?"

Murphy pulled out a handkerchief and mopped his face. "Who killed Santucci?"

"I don't know."

"Any ideas?"

"No."

"Did he have any enemies?"

"Obviously, at least one."

"C'mon, Margolis."

"How about that drink?"

"How about answering my questions?"

"How about asking me some that I know the answers to."

He smiled. "OK. How did you know Santucci?"

"He used to play in a band called Dementia. I watched them play in the clubs and we got to hanging out."

"Was this before or after the smack?"

"Before."

"When did he start using smack?"

"About two years ago."

"Where'd he get his money from?"

"I don't know."

"What happened to his band?"

"They split up."

"And the other members?"

"Most of them are around."

"What do they do?"

"I don't know. One of them plays with Zone and The Dangers."

"Where the hell do they get these names from? Zone and The Dangers. That kills me. Any hostilities when they broke up?"

"No, I don't think so."

"What do you know about Santucci's family?"

I shrugged. "They're out in New Jersey somewhere. His brother owns Sanka's in Hoboken."

He looked at me carefully. It was the look cops give you when they want to see if you're lying. They stare you straight in the eye and see if you can look back at them. My father used to play that game all the time, only we always ended up laughing.

I must have passed the test because Murphy continued. "Where'd Santucci get his drugs from?"

"I don't know. How about that drink?"

"How could you know a guy for so long and know so little about him?"

"I been asking myself the same question."

"Had you been to Santucci's before?"

"Yeah."

"How often?"

"Lots of times."

"Like what? Ten?"

"More."

"A hundred?"

"Maybe."

"Anything unusual this time?" I started to say something and he cut me off. "Besides the fact that he was dead."

I needed a drink. I couldn't go on too much longer

playing verbal volleyball with this guy. I just wanted them to leave me alone with my scotch. And there was only one way to get them to do that. "Yeah. There was something unusual."

Murphy raised his eyebrows, which made me think of Philips who had retreated back to the door. Philips didn't move.

"I saw someone coming out of the building when I got there."

"Did you get a good look at him?"

"I know who it was."

"Margolis! You might just get that drink after all. Who was it?"

"The Merk."

"The Merk?" I could tell that he knew who I was talking about. "The Merk? You saw The Merk coming out of Santucci's building?"

"Yup."

"Son of a bitch!" Murphy tossed me the scotch. I grabbed it and took a good long guzzle straight from the bottle and suddenly everything was tolerable.

"The Merk is a lieutenant for Gus Harper," Murphy said.

"I know," Philips said, and he took a few steps away from the door. "Are you sure it is The Merk?"

Murphy winked at me and smiled. I couldn't tell if it was because Philips had come back out of his corner or because he knew that my feet and fingers were beginning to tingle.

"Yeah, I'm sure."

"How close did you get to him?"

"I don't know. A hundred feet."

"Get a good look at him?"

"No."

"How'd you know it was him?"

"He's hard to miss."

"Why's that?"

"He's got a mohawk."

"Lots of them have mohawks."

"He has no left ear."

"Yeah, that's him." He seemed disappointed and he backed off again into his corner.

I took another good long pull from the bottle. Things were getting brighter by the moment.

"Did The Merk see you?" Murphy asked.

"I don't know."

"Which way did he go when he left Santucci's building?"

"I don't know. But I saw him again later outside Tompkins Park."

"How much later?"

"I don't know. Maybe an hour. Maybe two."

"What was he doing?"

"Just hanging out. Then I followed him to Avenue B where he was picked up by a limousine."

"Get the license plate?"

"No. Who's Gus Harper?"

Murphy stood up. "Margolis, I don't have to tell you that we ask the questions around here. You stick around for a few days. We're not finished with you yet." He followed Philips to the door but turned around before he went out. "Oh, and Margolis, get a job."

I sat on my bed and drank more scotch. Above the hum of the fan I heard the traffic on the Bowery. From somewhere off I heard a radio blasting. They would be break-dancing in the park now. In Florida the fishermen would be coming in for lunch. I heard Murphy's voice, "Does your father know you're a drunk?"

I drank more scotch.

It's easy to decide to quit drinking when you're drunk. I'd done it many times. You down that one last drink and you walk home feeling like a new man and thinking about your new life. When you get home you go to sleep without a nightcap just to show yourself how easy it is. But then you wake up in the morning, or in the early afternoon, and you know that only a drink can save you from the misery and the boredom of the day. You've got to make it past that. This morning I'd almost done that, and then those two cops had to walk into my life.

The bottle was still about half full. I put the bottle to my lips and I drank, and I didn't stop. I was sweating, my eyes were watering and my guts were burning, but I didn't stop until I threw the empty bottle down on the bed. It was like jumping off a cliff and waiting to land. I didn't have to wait long.

I got to the bathroom just in time. Kneeling in front of the toilet I vomited, and I sweated, and I cried. I felt as if I'd reached the end. There was nothing left except a hollow sickness in the pit of my stomach. It felt like death. My ears were ringing with the sound of Murphy's voice. "Does your father know you're a drunk?" I didn't want to be a drunk. I didn't want to be dead. And, on the bathroom floor, in the middle of the afternoon, I decided it was time to live.

Chapter 5

Jack's place had gotten worse since the last time I'd been there. There was just enough light to make out dimly the forms of people and objects scattered around the room. A couple of mattresses thrown on the floor were being used as couches and an old wooden crate turned upside down served as a coffee table. A little table by the door had a record player on it that was probably still broken. The curtain over the bathroom door had finally come down, and it lay in a bundle on the floor. So much for the privacy of shooting up in the bathroom. The air had the same stale smell, like that of a dog coming in from the rain, but at least it was cooler than it was outside.

Jack was sitting in his chair. He had always been a junkie. He started using the stuff back in the sixties when the East Village was filled with hippies. He still wore his hair long. About ten years ago some bikers smashed his face into a wall and he was missing a lot of teeth. Supposedly he had quit the stuff a few times, but not since I'd known him.

The first time I went to Jack's was with Tony. Jack was the only junkie then. The rest of us would just hang around his apartment and drink, or smoke, or snort. Slowly, and with no doing of Jack's, the junkies took over, or more of us became junkies, until it was all junkies except me and Leon. Leon dropped out quickly enough. I lasted another couple of months until I got tired of drinking by myself and being surrounded by zombies.

"Eddie, man, you never stop by," Jack said.

A figure moved from one of the mattresses and came

into the light. It was Little Danny. "Eddie. Eddie, man.
You hear about Tony?" He put his hand on my shoulder.
Little Danny was everybody's kid brother who somehow
had gotten mixed up with drugs. He was a pitiful junkie.
Being addicted to smack brought along never-ending pressure to keep yourself in supply; Little Danny couldn't take
the pressure and one of these days it was going to crack
him. He was short and skinny and wore round wire-rim
glasses. He wore his hair sort of long, like Jack, but it was
dark and stringy. He should have been a computer analyst,
but somehow he got into dope. He was as high as a kite.

"Yeah, I heard, Danny. I was the one who found him."

"You found him?"

Then a voice from the corner. "Jack, man, who is this
guy?"

"Don't worry, he's cool. This is Eddie. You know
these guys, Eddie?"

"Do you?"

I heard someone laugh and then say, "Yo! Ed-dee!" I
couldn't see, but I knew it was Curry.

"What's up, Curry?"

Then Jack said, "I think there's still some scotch here.
Under the sink or something."

"That's all right, Jack." I sat down on the floor with
my back against the door. It was as good a place to sit as
any. I felt wary eyes peering at me from the darkness. It
was all right if you weren't a junkie, just so long as you
were a drunk. But if you weren't a junkie or a drunk, then
you didn't belong here.

"Hey, Eddie, man!" Another familiar voice. This time
it was Willis. He was sitting somewhere near Curry. "You
remember there used to be a guy named Leon?"

That's how junkies were. As soon a you stopped hanging out they'd talk about you like you were dead. "Yeah,
sure."

"If you see that guy, tell him to go fuck himself."

I laughed.

"I asked the guy to lend me some bucks, you know. I
was good for it. I was gonna pay him back. You know

what he said to me, man? He told me to go take a fucking hike. If you see that guy, tell him to go fuck himself.''

"Yeah, sure, Willis. I'll tell him.''

"Yo, Jack, man, who is this guy?'' Somebody didn't like me. I waited for Jack to come to my defense again, but he said nothing.

Little Danny was on the floor now, leaning against Jack's chair. "You were the one who found him, Eddie?''

"Yeah, I found him.''

"Was he dead when you found him?''

"Dead as a doornail.''

"What'd they do? Shoot him?''

"Yeah.''

"Who killed him?''

"I don't know.''

Jack broke in. "Was it bad, Eddie?''

"It wasn't nice.''

"I seen a guy get shot once.'' It was Willis again. No one said anything so he continued. "It was a bloody fucking mess, man. I ain't never seen anything like it.''

"Shit, Willis,'' Curry challenged. "When did you ever see anybody get shot?''

"Couple of years ago. Up on Tenth Street.''

"You mean Trap?''

"No. This guy's name was Pete.''

"Do you guys know who The Merk is?'' I asked.

Nobody said anything. Maybe I was asking the wrong crowd. Maybe The Merk was their dealer or something. It was too late to turn back now. "I saw him leaving Tony's building just before I got there.''

"You think he did it?'' Jack asked.

"Of course he fucking did it,'' Curry said.

"Why would he kill Tony?'' I asked.

"The guy's a fucking asshole, that's why,'' Curry continued. "You see he doesn't have a left ear? You know what happened to it? You're not going to fucking believe this.''

"Try me.''

"He cut it off with his own fucking knife.''

"What for?"

"Ready for this? On a goddamned bet for a hundred dollars. He cut off his own fucking ear."

Jack was nodding. "That's right, Eddie. I've heard that."

"Can you believe that fucking shit?" Curry asked. "Fucking asshole cuts off his own ear for a hundred fucking dollars."

"Why would he kill Tony?" I asked.

"I don't know. Tony had been hanging with him," Jack said.

"Bullshit!" Curry broke in. "Tony hanging with The Merk? What, are you fucking crazy? You'd have to be nuts to hang out with that asshole. Tony was as scared of him as anybody else."

"Maybe, but he'd been hanging with him," Jack said.

"Why would he hang with The Merk?" I asked. "Did The Merk deal?"

"Jack! I don't like this guy!" It was that voice from the corner.

"I told you, he's cool." Then to me, "No, I don't think so. I think he was a pimp or something. I really don't know, Eddie."

"Jack," I asked, "do you think The Merk could have done it?"

"Hard to say."

"The cops say he works for a guy named Gus Harper."

"Shit, he talked to the fucking cops, man!" It was my friend from the corner. We ignored him.

"Yeah? That could be."

"Who's Gus Harper?"

"People say that Gus Harper runs all the drugs down here, but I been down here a long time and I ain't never seen or heard of anybody named Gus Harper."

"I heard of him," Little Danny said. "Somebody told me that he's the king of the East Village."

"That's a crock of shit," Willis said. "The dude runs a store over on C, that's all. I know who he is. He's some spic with a white man's name, that's all."

Jack shook his head. "I don't know what to tell you, Eddie. But stay away from The Merk, man. He's bad business."

"The cops think that I was trying to sell Tony dope."

Curry laughed. "Yeah, Eddie the dealer. Ed-dee!" He laughed some more. "What'd you tell them?"

"I told them that I didn't sell drugs but that you boys might be able to help them."

Curry laughed, but the guy in the corner couldn't take it anymore. "Jack, get him out of here before I kill him. It's not funny, man. Get the fuck out of here, you creep!"

Curry kept laughing and then nobody said anything for a while. I couldn't see, but I suspected that some of them were nodding out. Somebody outside walked by with a radio blasting salsa music. I listened to it as it moved down the street and finally blended into other city noises: the occasional car out on Allen Street, the high-pitched sound of a car alarm somewhere off in the distance. For a noisy city, it sure could be quiet sometimes.

I thought about the scotch Jack had offered me. I was still feeling a little queasy from my morning's over-consumption, and a little scotch would probably have helped a whole lot. Who would know if I took a small hit off the bottle? It was probably a bottle I had brought there years ago. Who would care if I had a drink?

"Hey, Eddie, man. Where'd they shoot him?" Willis, looking for details.

"In his apartment."

"No, man, I mean they shoot him in the head or what?" Willis, looking for gory details.

"Shit, Willis!" Jack said. "What's the matter with you?"

"Why'd they have to kill him?" Little Danny asked from the floor.

"Hey, Eddie, man." Willis wasn't finished.

"Yeah, what, Willis?"

"How about lending me some bucks? Just till Tuesday. I'm good for it, man."

"Take a hike, Willis."

That made Curry laugh.

"Shit, man. You and that fucking guy Leon. Both of you can go fuck yourselves."

"Why'd they have to kill him?" Little Danny asked.

I couldn't take it anymore. I got up to leave. "Don't get up, fellas." Jack and Little Danny said good-bye. Curry said my name and laughed just for the hell of it. It was hot outside, but I was happy to be out of there.

Out of habit I walked to The Pit, but when I got there I stopped at the door and looked inside. Saturday nights in New York always start a little later, but they go longer. The crowd was three deep at the bar and everyone was screaming trying to get Abraham's attention. Abraham was having a field day banging his stick on the bar and yelling at someone about something. Ivan was toward the back, just drinking a beer. He didn't even know where to start.

I caught a glimpse of Leon talking to a couple of girls. If I went in I would have a drink. It was that simple. I stepped out of the doorway and leaned against the outside wall to watch the crowd on Avenue A. What do you do with yourself when you don't drink? What do you do at night? What do you ever do? It seemed like all of a sudden I had all of this free time on my hands. What did it mean for time to be free anyway? It meant that it was mine to do what I wanted with. I wanted to drink. No, it was the fact that I was not drinking that gave me all of this free time. What did most people do? They had jobs. They had wives and kids. They had money to burn. What did I have? Lots of free time and a raging desire for a Johnnie Walker Red on the rocks.

The Merk was out there again, in the same spot with his friends. There were a few girls standing in front of them playing with knives. Lovely girls. I wondered why Philips and Murphy hadn't picked him up yet. I surveyed the street for possible undercover cops and found one down near the pizza parlor on the corner of Eighth Street. He wore a a pair of clean blue jeans and a muscle shirt. He might have passed as another denizen of Avenue A except that he had a neatly trimmed mustache. Nobody on Av-

enue A had a mustache. And nobody on Avenue A was
neatly trimmed.

A bottle cap came flying out of The Pit and landed in
the street. A punk standing there turned around and looked
at me. His head had been shaved and he wore about four
different kinds of earrings in each ear. His shirt said,
"Fuck art, let's dance."

"Did you throw that, man?" He had one of those prac-
ticed whiny punk voices.

"No, I don't think so."

"Are you sure?"

Then I noticed that The Merk had started to move. He was
turning the corner down Seventh Street as he had the night
before. I watched the cop, but he didn't move. He didn't
even seem to notice. I'd give him thirty seconds, and I
started counting.

"Man, I'm talking to you," the punk said.

I laughed.

"Hey, it's not funny, man. I got to know."

Thirty seconds were up and the cop hadn't moved. He
wasn't tailing The Merk. So suddenly I was. I left the
punk to his important business of figuring out who threw
the bottle cap and headed for the corner. Seventh Street
was crowded so I stayed on the park side.

The Merk was about halfway down the block when he
turned into the park. I didn't like that. He could have gone
into the park from where he had been sitting. There was a
break in the stone wall where he had entered, and I
stopped and looked into the park. I could make out his
figure, bobbing along on a path heading toward the north-
west corner of the deserted park. I followed him.

They were good. They were on top of me before I even
heard them coming over the railing. I went down hard and
I felt the sweet warm taste of blood in my mouth. One of
them sat on my back and held my arms behind me. The
other called out to The Merk. The one who was holding
me pushed one of my arms up hard against my back. It felt
like it was going to break.

"Get up, motherfucker."

I got up slowly. He was still holding my arm. I heard the click of a switchblade and then saw the eight-inch blade.

"Let go of my arm."

"Go ahead, motherfucker. Try to get away." I felt the point of the knife in my neck.

"Let go of my arm."

He laughed and pulled me off the path into the shadows. I spit blood. The Merk had come up to us now and they turned me to face him. His mohawk stuck up about six inches, so he was even shorter than he seemed. He had two gold earrings in his right ear. His left side was just a gruesome hole.

"What da fuck are you doin', man?" His mouth hardly moved when he spoke, as if the words were coming from his stomach.

"Tell him to let go of my arm."

"Listen, you fuck. What da fuck do you think you're doin'?"

"Shit, he's breaking my fucking arm!"

The Merk's fist came up hard and fast. It was small but made of steel and he hit me right under the rib cage. I doubled over, only to get caught by his foot on my chin. As I went down I had the perverse feeling of satisfaction that I had gotten the guy to let go of my arm.

I rolled over and sat up. I stretched my arm. It didn't feel broken, but it hurt like hell. I spit more blood.

"Get him up," The Merk said.

They got me up.

"Now listen to me, fuckface. You think I killed Santucci, don't you?"

"What do you care what I think?"

"I don't care what you think. I care what you tell the pigs. You told them I was there."

"Weren't you?"

"Let me tell you something, fuck. I didn't kill Santucci. He was dead when I got there. Just like he was dead when you got there."

"So what are you worried about?"

"The fucking pigs, that's what I'm worried about. I can't have fucks like you pointing fingers at me and following me around. It's bad for business."

"Don't flatter yourself. Nobody's following you."

He hit me again, in the same spot, but this time I didn't go down. I just spit more blood.

"You're so busy following me, you don't even know the score, man."

"Yeah, well so educate me."

"I didn't kill Santucci. Tell that to your pig friends. Santucci was killed by the Chinese."

"The Chinese? What Chinese? Why . . ." But I didn't get to finish.

A gun fired. I'd always wondered what it was like to get shot. I hoped I wouldn't die right away. I wanted to experience it. I waited to feel the pain.

Then The Merk sat down. Just like that. Slowly he leaned forward until his forehead was touching the hard pavement. If it weren't for the mohawk he might have looked like a Moslem praying. His two friends had disappeared. There were just me and The Merk.

Me and The Merk, and one undercover cop with a mustache and a gun to my head.

"One move and you're a dead asshole. Now let's get those hands up. OK. That's good." He gave me a patdown, then pulled my arms down and slapped a pair of handcuffs on me.

"What's going on?"

He didn't say anything but just dragged me out of the park onto Seventh Street where a police car was waiting for us. A small crowd had already gathered. He threw me in the backseat. I heard him say to a uniformed cop, "There's another one in there. You better get an ambulance."

The undercover cop got in on the passenger side of the front seat and a uniformed cop got behind the wheel, the siren started and we were off.

"Where are we going?"

No answer.

"What the hell is going on? Where the hell are we going?"

The undercover cop turned around. "Don't ask so many questions, kid. We're taking you to your apartment so you can have a chat with Murphy. Sit back and enjoy the ride and think about how lucky you are that you're alive."

And I did just that.

Chapter 6

The elevator was still broken and my body was beginning to ache from my run-in with The Merk. After three flights I had to stop and rest, and I asked them to take the handcuffs off. The undercover cop with the mustache pushed me onward and told me it was my own damn fault. I didn't know if he was talking about the handcuffs or the elevator.

The door was open when we got upstairs and they pushed me inside. The place was a wreck. All of the shelves and closets had been emptied and piled in the middle of the floor and some cop I had never seen before was emptying my drawers. I stared at all my worldly possessions piled in a big heap, as if they were about to be hauled off to the dump: books, records, fishing rods, an old Instamatic camera, cassettes, papers, a flashlight, clothes, tools, notebooks, calendars, postcards. Maybe they'd be doing me a favor if they took them to the dump.

Murphy was sitting in the armchair and talking on the telephone. When he saw me his face lit up with a big grin. He grunted something into the phone and hung up. "Margolis! The Cuban Jew! We've been waiting for you!"

"What the hell's going on?"

Murphy looked around dubiously and shrugged his shoulders. "You're under arrest. And we're searching your apartment."

"How'd you get in here?"

"We broke in."

"Just like that, huh?"

"Just like that. What are you going to do, call the cops?"

Everyone laughed.

"What am I under arrest for?"

Murphy frowned casually. "Just murder. You might want to call your lawyer."

"I don't have a lawyer. I've already told you everything I know. Now what the fuck do you want from me?"

"Relax, Margolis. We've got a lot to talk about."

"Can't you at least take these things off?"

The telephone rang and Murphy picked it up like this was his office. He held the receiver to his chest and said, "Yeah, sure. Jimmy, take the cuffs off." Then he spoke into the phone. "Murphy here."

Jimmy was the undercover cop with the mustache. He took the cuffs off and I sat down on the bed, which had been stripped of its sheets. The fan felt good. The other cop, who had been there when we walked in, was a short little guy with narrow shoulders. He was going through the drawers like a mouse looking for cheese. Then there was the uniformed cop, the driver. He stood near the doorway looking uncomfortable.

Murphy slammed down the phone and stared at me. "The Merk is dead. DOA."

"That's a shame."

"It is a shame. We had one decent lead on Gus Harper and you wasted him."

"I wasted him?"

"What were you doing? Getting him back for Santucci?"

"You don't know what you're talking about."

"What were you doing in the park anyway?"

I told him briefly about being jumped and beaten.

"You don't look too bad," he said.

"I feel like shit."

"You get a good look at the guys who jumped you?"

"No."

No one said anything for a while. Then Murphy picked up a piece of paper from his lap. It looked vaguely familiar. He read:

Sometimes in the madness of the afternoon
I forget how much I miss our whispers

Bouncing in the morning darkness
Like clandestine little sisters.

I fell back on the bed and stared at the ceiling. Why couldn't The Merk have killed me? Death would have been better than having my adolescent efforts at poetry read back to me by a big ugly pig. Murphy read on:

And when we start to cry and fight
She asks me if she should stay
The world is what it is
Hooray for Gray!''

They all clapped. I needed a drink more than anything in the world. ''You want to hear more?'' Murphy asked.

I stared at the ceiling. ''No.''

''It's yours, isn't it?''

''So what?''

''You didn't tell me you were a poet.''

''I'm not. I haven't written anything in years.''

''But you used to write.''

''Who didn't?''

''I didn't. Santucci was a poet too, wasn't he?''

''He wrote lyrics.''

''And you were friends.''

''So what?''

''So you were both poets and you were friends.''

''So what?''

''You're a queer, aren't you?''

''Jesus Christ!'' I sat up.

''I think you're a queer.''

''I don't give a shit what you think.''

''How come you're not drinking, Margolis?''

''I don't feel like it.''

''Did you quit?''

''I don't know. I'll tell you in a few days.''

He frowned and nodded his head. ''Tell me about Florida, Margolis.''

''It's a state in the South with a lot of sun.''

"When did you come to New York?"

"What is this?"

"Was your father a good agent?"

"He was the best."

"What about your mother?"

"She died when I was six. What is this? What do you care about all this?"

"I don't care. I'm just trying to figure you out, that's all."

"Well, good luck."

"How long have you been out of work?"

"Forever."

"Forever?"

"I had a job with a magazine for a while, but I quit."

"Why'd you quit?"

"I hated it."

"You go to college?"

"In Florida, for one semester."

"You quit that too?"

"Yeah, so what?"

Murphy put his feet up on the coffee table and put his hands behind his head. "You're a real loser, you know that?"

"Why don't you leave me alone?"

"I can't. You saw The Merk leaving Santucci's building when you got there, right?"

I got up and went to the kitchen area to make coffee.

"Hey, Margolis, I'm talking to you."

"I'm listening."

"Did you or didn't you see The Merk leaving Santucci's building?"

"Yeah, I did."

"By the front door?"

"No, he jumped out the window," I said, and instantly regretted my sarcasm.

"Well, somebody did."

I ignored him and started scooping out coffee.

"Margolis, let me explain something to you. There's a little old lady who lives downstairs from Santucci's apartment. I think she's been there since the turn of the century. She's wacko, but she loves cops.''

"She must be wacko."

"She was there last night when Santucci was killed. You know what she says?''

The problem with coffee was that I was used to having it with a shot of scotch in it.

"She says that Santucci had *three* visitors last night. First, someone went in and shot him. That person left by the front door. Then someone else went in for a minute and left by the front door. Finally, someone went in and left by jumping out the fucking window. Can you believe that?''

It was taking an awful long time for the water to boil.

"Well, Margolis? What do you think?''

"So The Merk went in and shot him, and someone came in after me and jumped out the window.''

"Good try.''

"Why not?''

"Because The Merk didn't kill Santucci.''

"How do you know?''

"It was too messy. It was done by an amateur. The Merk is a pro. He wouldn't have made such a mess of it. And he wouldn't have been seen coming out of the building.''

"So what are you saying?''

"I'm saying that either you jumped out the window or you killed Santucci.''

I checked the water. Not even close. "C'mon, if I killed Santucci, then that ruins your theory that I killed The Merk because I thought he killed Santucci.''

Murphy nodded. "Good point. You mean you jumped out the window. And killed The Merk.''

"Maybe I climbed out the window but didn't kill anybody.''

"Ah! Now we're getting somewhere. You climbed out the window.''

The water was steaming, but not boiling.

"Didn't you, Margolis?''

Maybe if I just stopped talking, they would go away.

"Margolis, talk to me. Why'd you climb out the window?"

I turned and faced him, but I didn't say anything.

"Was it because you were scared of getting caught with drugs on you?"

"That again?"

"C'mon, Margolis," he said softly. "What'd you jump out the window for? I just want to know."

"You just want to know?"

"I just want to know."

"I was scared."

"Scared? You don't seem like the type that scares easy."

"Maybe I don't like dead bodies."

"Margolis, dead bodies don't bother you. Most people, when they find a stiff, it takes a week until you can drag them out of the station. Santucci was shot up pretty bad. I don't think it bothered you at all."

"I've seen it before."

The water finally came to a boil and I poured it carefully through the filter, breathing in the steam and the smell of coffee. Murphy was staring at me, waiting for an explanation, so I gave it to him.

"Once I was out fishing with my father and some Columbian smugglers kidnapped us. They wanted to hold us for ransom for their friends who my father had thrown in jail. There were four of them. They dragged us onto their boat and took off for the high seas. My father got a gun away from one of them and killed him and one other. The other two surrendered."

Murphy nodded. "Heavy stuff for a kid. How old were you?"

"Eleven. I watched one of them die. My father tied the two who had surrendered to the bow of the boat so he could keep an eye on them while he drove. The other two he put in the cabin and told me to keep an eye on them just in case they tried anything. One was dead already. The other just bled all over the boat. He was dead by the time we got to port."

Murphy gazed up at the ceiling. "My kid'll be eleven next month."

"Don't take him fishing."

"Margolis, I want to ask you one more time. How come you jumped out the window?"

"I don't know. Probably because I was drunk."

He laughed. "That's the best answer you've given me all day. But I got another problem. If you didn't kill Santucci, and The Merk didn't kill Santucci, then who did?"

"The Merk said it was the Chinese."

"The Chinese? What Chinese?"

"I don't know. He was shot before I could ask him."

"He told you this just now, between punches?"

"Yup."

Murphy got up out of his chair and started to pace. "The Chinese, huh? Jimmy? Any ideas?"

"Could be anything. Besides, they all look alike."

The uniformed cop laughed.

"Hey, Margolis, that coffee smells good. Aren't you going to offer me some?"

"No."

"You're damned unfriendly Margolis."

"I don't like being under arrest. By the way, who did I kill again? I keep forgetting?"

"You know, Margolis, I don't think you killed Santucci. I wasn't sure when I first got here, but now I am."

"So now you think I killed The Merk?"

"You know, it's hotter than hell in here."

"Buy me an air conditioner."

I poured the coffee into a mug and took that ever-needed first sip. It tasted like coffee with no booze. That's how most people drank it. Maybe I could get used to it. I sat in the big armchair where Murphy had been sitting. After all, it was still my apartment.

"OK, Margolis. I'm unarresting you."

"Thanks."

"Anyway, the Santucci case is up on the shelf."

"On the shelf, what for?"

"We did all we could do, for a junkie."

"One day? That's all he gets?"

"The point is we don't have the time or the manpower to track down the murderer of every lousy junkie that gets his head blown off. This is New York, and if you're gonna get killed, well, you better be a doctor or a lawyer. Otherwise, forget it."

He stood behind me and looked out the window. "That's quite a view you got here, Margolis. I knew you jumped out the window. It's the only way this thing makes sense. I just came here to shake you up a little to see what you were hiding. Homicide doesn't give a fuck about Santucci. I don't know what the hell Philips got involved for. The only reason I'm here is to see if I can stumble onto something bigger. You see what I'm saying, Margolis?"

"Not exactly."

He walked back around to the center of the room. "See, I don't know if The Merk had anything to do with Santucci, but I'm going to look into it. But I'm not after Santucci's killer unless it happens to be a big fish, like Gus Harper, or someone like that."

He didn't say anything until I looked at him. Then with a slight wink he said, "That doesn't mean that if somebody found out who killed Santucci we wouldn't do anything about it."

I started to say something, but he held up his hand.

"Now I'm not asking you to go out and play detective. Let's get this straight. You start dicking around and I'll have another dead body on my hands. All I'm saying is that if, in your natural state of unemployment, you're hanging around or you happen to hear something of interest, well, let me know. Maybe we can help each other out."

I took a good long sip of coffee.

"Are you going to Santucci's funeral?" Murphy asked.

I shrugged.

"It's in New Jersey. I thought you ought to know. After all, he was your friend."

I nodded.

"Oh, and good luck with the booze, Margolis."

That was it. They left me to my cup of coffee, my torn-apart room and my aching body.

It was midnight, and I was sober. I drank more coffee. I cleaned up the mess in the middle of the room. I went downstairs to look for Holly, but she wasn't there. None of the girls had seen her. I climbed the seven flights back up to my apartment and took a bath. At around two in the morning I got into bed.

I spent the night tossing around and thinking about Columbians and cops and Tony. The cops were putting Tony's case on the shelf. One day was all he got. He was a junkie, so it wasn't supposed to matter. And if someone had killed a drunk like me, it wouldn't have mattered either. But I wasn't a drunk anymore, and Tony was dead. I had to find his killer. I owed it to Tony. And I owed it to myself. And only when the first splinter of light found its way into my dark apartment did I fall into a long and peaceful sleep.

Chapter 7

Funerals are as trivial as death is profound.

When my mother died, my family was terrified because all I wanted to do was sit by myself in my room. They dragged me out so that all of my aunts and uncles could show me how sorry they felt for me. And at the funeral there were all these people I didn't know, crying for my mother. I felt cheated, as if somehow their grief deprived me of my own.

On the beginning of my third full day of being sober I took a PATH train to Newark, New Jersey, to go to Tony's funeral. I had gotten a late start as it was, and between that and a mix-up in the train schedule, the ceremony was almost over by the time I got there. I slid into a pew in the back next to two old women. They were arguing over Tony's age. I leaned over and told them that he had been twenty-four, not because I was sure but to shut them up. It didn't work. They proceeded to cross-examine me to find out who I was, how I knew Tony, how old *I* was and if, with a series of mysterious and shameful glances at the pulpit, I knew "who did it." My answers didn't satisfy them, so finally I put a finger to my lips and pointed up front to indicate that I wanted to listen. One of them actually waved me off as if I were being silly.

I leaned forward with my chin on my hands and tried to listen to the sermon. In spite of myself, I found the chatter in my pew interesting.

"Tony was by his second wife," the far one was saying. "She passed away about five years ago."

"It's a terrible thing."

Then from the pulpit, "How is it that one of God's creatures can be so unfairly deprived of life at such an early age? Perhaps only God Himself can understand such seemingly senseless and untimely death. . . ."

"Two wives he's outlived now, and now this. And the older son, running around with that . . . that young blonde. I saw him kiss her right there in front of everyone. His wife and kids right there. Like the whole world didn't know what was going on."

"It's a terrible thing."

". . . help them in their lonely hours to find strength . . ."

"You know, I wouldn't be the least bit surprised if it was someone in this very church who did it."

"Oh Helen! Really!"

"The way that family carries on!"

When the service was over I stood up to let the two old chatterboxes out and then sat down again to watch the people. There were about fifty altogether. Mostly older people, in their sixties and seventies. There were no children. I had heard no crying, and although the faces were solemn, it was that solemn expression people wear when they hear of somebody else's misfortune.

Suddenly I saw Gloria among the unfamiliar faces. I almost didn't recognize her. She had put on some weight, which filled out her face and her figure in a healthy way, and her blond hair, instead of being short and spiked, had grown in, and she wore it up and back, away from her face and ears. She wore a black dress that would have been conservative if it had been just a little bit longer and when I looked up again she was staring at me, having caught me eyeing her legs.

"Eddie!" I stood up and took her hands as she came up and kissed me. "Thank you for coming," she said.

"It's a terrible thing," I heard myself say.

Her mouth was full and, as always, slightly puckered, and her eyes were puffy, not from crying but because her eyes were always puffy.

"Are you coming to the cemetery, Eddie?"

"I wasn't planning on it."

"Why don't you come? You can ride in my car. And you can come to the reception afterward."

"I hadn't realized that you were still so friendly with Tony."

She let go of my hand and went rummaging through her purse for something. "I wasn't that much. But I stayed pretty close to the family. It's horrible, what happened, Eddie."

"I know. Are you sure it's all right if I come?"

"Of course, c'mon." She pulled a pair of dark sunglasses from her purse and then grabbed my hand and dragged me out into the blinding New Jersey sun.

"Wait here, I'll go get the car." And she left me.

If you put New York City in a sifter and shook out all of the fun and beautiful things, so that only the unbearable grime was left, you would have Newark, New Jersey. The heat was ridiculous and in my sports coat and tie I was sweating uncontrollably. The block was lined with drab brick buildings with broken windows and FOR SALE signs. The street was congested with dirty trucks and buses emitting foul fumes. It was a living nightmare. A hearse pulled up to the curb in front of me, and behind that, a pair of limousines, and then the other cars. There was a red Mustang with tinted windows about halfway back in the line of cars. The door opened on the driver's side, and Gloria popped out and waved to me. She had her sunglasses on and was smoking a cigarette, and she suddenly looked different. She wasn't just a little punk kid from Chicago. Maybe she had changed a lot since the days of Tony, or maybe I had never really known her at all.

I walked over to the car and got in on the passenger side. It was air-conditioned!

"Nice car."

"Thanks. Sorry I took so long. It was only a block away, but, boy, the traffic is horrible."

The procession started to move, and we went creeping along the filthy, sweltering avenues. I realized that this was the first time I'd been out of New York in over a year.

A year to get out of New York, and where did I go?
Newark, New Jersey.

"You look different, Eddie," she said as soon as we
started moving.

"So do you."

"I mean you look older. What have you been doing
with yourself?"

"Not much."

"You see any of the old crowd?"

"Yeah, sometimes. I don't hang out at the clubs much
anymore."

"Not even CBGB's?"

"No."

"Are you working?"

"No."

"So what are you doing with yourself?"

"Like I said, not much."

"It's good to see you again, Eddie."

"It's good to see you too."

"Is it, really?"

"Yeah, really."

"I don't know. For some reason I always thought you
didn't like me."

"I always liked you. I guess I was a little pissed off that
you were always Tony's girl friend."

The pucker of her lips became exaggerated. "Remember
the time that you, Tony and I went to Coney Island?"

"Sure."

"Remember you won that big stuffed lion for me?"

"Yeah."

"I still have that, you know."

"No kidding?"

"It's sad what happened to Tony, Eddie."

"I know."

"No, I mean with the drugs."

"Oh."

"He used to be so alive and so with it. And his band
and his music, I think they were really good. Not just

because we knew them, but because they were really good. Everyone thought they were good. Remember?''

"Yeah."

"It really hurt his family too. Frank, that's his brother, was really torn up. They all wanted so much for Tony."

We drove for a while without saying anything. We had left the hard-core part of the city and were now on a suburban street with big wooden two-family houses on both sides. They weren't the newest houses around, but they had porches and little yards and there were toys and little kids around.

"Gloria, I want to find out who killed Tony."

She stomped out her cigarette in the ashtray and lit another one. "Don't you think you ought to leave that for the police?"

"The police aren't going to do anything. They already told me so."

"So what are you going to do?"

"I don't know yet."

"If you ask me, Eddie, it was probably one of those junkie friends of his or something. You know how junkies are."

"Yeah, but I think it might be something bigger than that. When was the last time you saw him?"

"Oh, I don't know, a few months ago I guess. We'd meet for a drink every once in a while."

"Did he tell you anything about what was going on last time you saw him?"

"What do you mean?"

"Did he mention a guy named The Merk?"

"No."

"Gus Harper?"

"No."

"Do you know where he got his drugs from?"

"No."

"How about his money?"

"I don't know, Eddie."

I sighed and looked out the window. A house was being

painted. A lawn was being cut. A car was being washed. This was suburbia.

"I'm sorry, Eddie. I just really don't know anything about him anymore."

"It's sad how little we knew about him. What about his family? Would they know anything?"

"No. Tony stopped talking to them over a year ago. It's hard to say this, Eddie, but I think that as far as they were concerned, Tony was already dead. Frank and I have become very good friends."

"Oh, yeah? How good?"

"He's married, Eddie. And has two kids."

"You think Frank would mind if I talked to him about Tony?"

"You mean about who killed him?"

"Yeah."

"I don't think it would be a good idea, Eddie. They're a pretty tight family and they don't know you."

"Well, maybe I'll just have a little chat with him."

"Eddie! Listen to me. I brought you here, now you have to behave. I should have warned you, it's a *very difficult* family. Believe me."

"What do you mean, difficult?"

"They do things their own way. I don't think they'd like some outsider sticking his nose in the family business. Most people know enough not to mess with them."

"What are you saying? Are they mob or something?"

"No. I mean I think Frank may have connections, but they're not the Mafia or anything. I think he has to pay some people off every once in a while for his liquor license at the club, and stuff like that."

The procession pulled into the cemetery and we started a long, slow tour of cemetery streets. "I'll bet you Frank has some idea who did it," I said.

"Eddie, would you lay off before you—"

"—end up like Tony?"

She was stunned. "No. That's not what I was going to say. I was going to say you should stop before you make a fool of yourself."

When we stopped I went to get out of the car, but Gloria
grabbed my arm.

"Eddie?"

"What."

"It's good to see you again."

"Yeah, it's good to see you too."

Tony's father lived in a large and secluded brick house
somewhere in Englewood Cliffs. The lawn was impeccably
kept and even though we already sat in an air-conditioned
car, it seemed as if everything got cooler as soon as we
pulled into the drive. Large oaks and elms were scattered
about the lawn, covering the grass with deep, dark shadows. The walls surrounding the yard were covered with
soft green ivy that almost disguised the barbed wire running along the top of the wall. As we drove up the white
pebbled driveway I realized just how rich Tony's family
was, and it bothered me that he'd come from such wealth
and had died a junkie with five thousand dollars in his
shoe. The driveway ended in a large parking area with a
fountain in the middle, and Gloria pulled her Mustang in
among the limousines and the Cadillacs.

Inside was a house to match the lawn. We entered into a
large foyer with the requisite high ceiling and crystal
chandelier. It was a big empty-looking room with a marble
floor and strange ornaments tucked away in the corners. A
knight's full suit of armor stood off to one side in shiny
silver and gray. A butler greeted us at the door, and we
were brought down a long wide hallway and through a
large set of double doors into the main room where the
reception was. It was slightly shocking to walk into a room
that big. From the outside the house had looked large, but
not large enough to hold a football field. There were only
about twenty or thirty people, and that made the room
seem even bigger. There was a large semicircular table in
the middle filled with food and booze. Smaller tables were
set off to the side for people to sit at.

Gloria had pointed out Frank to me at the cemetery and
we saw him now standing near the booze with a glass in

his hand. His black suit fit him perfectly and his shoes sparkled against the rich white carpet. His straight black hair was combed neatly over the top of his head in an almost-successful attempt to hide a small bald spot. His face was pale and he had green eyes that seemed to focus intently on whatever he happened to be looking at. Right now he was focusing them on, of all people, one of the chatterboxes from the church, and from the way she was smiling and nodding her head I could tell that he was charming her to death.

He looked up at me and Gloria when we walked in, and I knew then that he and Gloria were more than friends. He excused himself from the chatterbox and met us halfway across the room.

"Frank, this is Eddie Margolis," Gloria said. "He was a friend of Tony's. This is Frank Santucci, Tony's brother."

We shook hands. For half-brothers there was a close resemblance. He looked the way Tony might have if he hadn't gotten into drugs.

"I'm real sorry about Tony," I said.

"Thank you. We all are. It was a horrible blow." His eyes focused on me and I watched them carefully. It was as if he were talking with his eyes. He was Tony's older brother and I was a friend of Tony's. His eyes said that meant that he was my older brother. "It was nice of you to come, Eddie."

"He was a good person, Frank."

"Yeah, I know. He was mixed up and confused, but I know he was a good person inside and I loved him."

I stood there awkwardly not knowing what to say.

"Weren't you the one who found him?" Frank asked finally.

"Yeah, that was me."

"It must have been horrible."

I nodded. "Yeah, it was pretty bad. It's a shame."

"Well, Eddie, have something to eat. Gloria, make sure he gets something to drink too, all right?" And he wandered off to go focus his green eyes on someone else.

Gloria led me to the big table where a man in a chef's

hat made me a sandwich. With a constant eye on the Chivas Regal, I ordered a ginger ale on the rocks. We took our own little table and Gloria smoked three cigarettes while I ate my sandwich.

"I'd like to meet Tony's father."

"Oh, he's around somewhere. I saw him a few minutes ago. He's really old, Eddie. It's sad. Frank says that he's not even sure if the old man understands that Tony's dead."

"He's senile?"

"He's pretty old, Eddie."

"What does he do that he has all this money?"

"Well, he's retired now. But he ran a few businesses. Mostly importing, I think. Eddie, I'll be back in a minute."

She left me and made a beeline for Frank. I watched his eyes turn and focus on her. She said something and they laughed. He grabbed her hand and squeezed it. They laughed some more. I had seen enough.

I finished my ginger ale and got up and asked one of the servants for a road map to the bathroom. He smiled and pointed down a hallway I hadn't seen before. "Third door to the right."

It was a big hallway, lavishly decorated with large oil paintings and sprinkled with comfortable-looking chairs and couches along the way, in case you got tired. It was long enough so that you might need them. All of the doors led off to the right, and just as I was a few steps from the second door, it opened, and I found myself face to face with an old man. It had to be Tony's father.

"Hello, Mr. Santucci. My name is Eddie Margolis. I was a friend of Tony's."

"Yes?" He held on to the door with one hand and I peeked past him into the room. It was a large study packed with books and furniture and a big mahogany desk right in the middle. It looked like a haven for an old man and I wondered if perhaps he felt the same way I did about funerals. "You have a beautiful house, Mr. Santucci."

His face gave no hint of what he was thinking. "Have you seen the garden, Mr. . . . ."

"Margolis. You can call me Eddie. No, I haven't seen the garden."

"You haven't seen the garden?"

"No, sir."

"Come, I'll show you the garden." I followed him down the hallway and through several doors and rooms until we finally ended up in the backyard. At least I thought it was the backyard, but I'd totally lost my sense of direction.

We followed a path around the trees and gardens and walked over a small wooden bridge that crossed a lively little creek. At last we came to the vegetable garden, and I followed patiently as he pointed out his tomato plants, his carrots, his green beans and a host of other vegetables and herbs, and, finally, his grapevines. A little white iron bench sat just outside the garden, shaded by a large weeping willow. He sat down to catch his breath and told me to do the same.

We sat in silence for a few minutes. Then he said, "What are you doing here?"

"I came with Gloria."

"Yes, I know."

"Mr. Santucci?"

"Yes?"

"Do you know that Tony's dead?"

He looked at me. "Yes, sometimes I know that."

More silence.

"You'll forgive me, Mr. . . ."

"Eddie."

"Mr. Eddie, but to me Tony died years ago. As soon as he started putting that junk in his veins. He was a no-good son of a bitch."

I didn't know what to say so I said nothing.

"How about you?" he asked. "Do you do that stuff?"

"No."

"You were friends with him, though."

"Tony was a good person, Mr. Santucci."

"Yes? Then why'd you let him do that to himself?"

"I could ask you the same question."

He snorted. "People don't usually talk to me like that, Mr. Eddie."

"Mr. Santucci, I want to find out who killed your son."

I listened to him breathing quietly. I listened to the birds chirping at the heat, and to the faraway sound of traffic drifting over the walls from another world.

"I do too, Mr. Eddie." He snorted again. "You have an interesting way about you, Mr. Eddie. I think you may just find out who killed Tony. Promise me you will."

"Sure."

"You know, when you get old like me, your interests in the world start to change. I don't care much for business anymore. I find I spend a lot of time wishing that the world had more compassion in it. Do you collect stamps?"

"No, sir."

I looked up and noticed Frank coming up the walk. When he had gotten within hearing distance Mr. Santucci said, "It's a shame you don't collect stamps. You'll have to stop by and take a look at my collection sometime. Hello, Frank."

Gloria lived down in the Village, but she wasn't going home yet. She told me she would give me a ride to the George Washington Bridge where I could catch a bus back to New York. As we walked out of the house into the driveway she caught me staring at her and smiling.

"What are you smiling at?"

"I don't know. I'm just trying to figure it all out. I mean Frank and Tony seem like such different people. Did Tony know about you and Frank?"

"Eddie, I told you. We're just friends. He's like a brother to me."

"Bullshit, Gloria. You're not fooling anybody."

We were at her car and she stood there staring at the house. "Is it really that obvious?"

I nodded.

"No, Tony didn't know. But I don't think he would have minded."

"Yeah, it's probably why he went and got himself shot."

She started to walk away, but I grabbed her arm. "Hey, where'd you get that sense of humor?"

"There's nothing funny about a funeral, Eddie."

"Maybe not, but you and Frank sure seemed to be having a good—"

She stopped me in mid-sentence with a slap in the face. We stood in the hot sun staring at each other and I felt my cheek start to sting. Finally I smiled and said, "I'll be seeing you, Gloria." It was a long walk to the George Washington Bridge, but I took my jacket and tie off and let myself work up a good sweat.

Chapter 8

The women wore light-colored cotton dresses and fanned themselves with yesterday's *El Diario*. They sat on the stoops of their neighbors' building and talked about the weather and the price of meat. Sometimes they would drink iced tea and watch their barefooted children run through the spray of an open fire hydrant. Every once in a while they would yell out to the little one to look out for a car.

The men came home from work—hot, dirty and tired. One of them had hit the numbers and bought beers at the corner deli. They stood on the sidewalks near the women, but off by themselves, and they'd drink their beer and throw an occasional stray ball back into the street for the children. There were nights when the men got drunk and loud, and sometimes they'd fight with their wives, but the children learned to sleep through that.

It was a safe block.

Then a few of the men got laid off from work and couldn't pay their rent. The drunk super didn't mind, but when the winter came there was no heat. The people from the City came, a man and a woman, and looked around. The woman spoke Spanish, and she asked a few questions and took notes in a big red notebook. She said that the City would talk to the landlord. The heat came on, but only for a few weeks. And then it was January.

This time only the man came from the City. He walked around the apartments and made sure that all of the windows were closed. He told one of the children who spoke English that he would talk to the landlord again and would get the heat turned on. The child told her mother and the man left. The children ran out and played in the snow, happy that soon they would have heat again. But the mothers sat inside wrapped in blankets and waited.

Some of the families moved out. They moved to Brooklyn or Queens, or the Bronx. The families that didn't have the money to move watched as apartments became empty and the buildings began to deteriorate. Junkies started to move onto the block.

One morning on their way to school the children found a dead junkie on the street. When the summer came they weren't allowed to play in the street anymore. The men and the women talked. You couldn't raise a child right anymore. Everyone moved out but the junkies, and the junkies didn't care when the electricity was turned off.

When the dealers took over they brought knives and guns. Even the police were afraid to walk down the block. They would walk in fours and fives, or drive down in their cars. They never did anything, except call an ambulance when they found a body they couldn't ignore. But nobody complained because nobody cared.

One day in some back City office, a lonely clerk discovered the unpaid real estate taxes. He had never heard of Avenue B. He made a few phone calls and shuffled a few papers. He brought the papers to his boss who approved them without looking at them and then the clerk sent them to the courthouse. A sleepy judge signed the papers and suddenly the City owned a block it had never seen. The dealers and the junkies remained, undisturbed.

A year or so passed. Then some City politician decided that something had to be done about the drug problem. The work crews arrived early in the morning before the dealers and junkies were awake. They gutted the buildings and they filled the doors and windows with bricks. Glassy-eyed junkies stumbled out from the corners and the basements like cockroaches disturbed by the exterminator's spray. The politician had his picture taken on the steps where the women used to sit. The steps now led to a brick wall.

For a few years the block was silent and empty. It was a safe block again.

Eli Frances was a clothing designer whose livelihood depended on his ability to start a trend. He bought one of the buildings on the block, paid the back taxes and the electric bills, and opened a club called The Frontier. Just in case people were afraid that it was a club for low-life, he charged twenty dollars at the door and put two guards armed with baseball bats in the lobby.

It was easy to find The Frontier. All you had to do was walk down the street and listen for the music. When you got to the building you knocked on the door and waited. After a few seconds the door would open and either you got to pay twenty bucks or you got hit in the head with a baseball bat. I guess for some people that was exciting.

It was still hot that Thursday night when I went to see Sam play with Zone and the Dangers at The Frontier.

Sam had been the drummer for Dementia. Tony had discovered Sam playing a snare drum in a square down on Wall Street during lunchtime. There was a crowd of about a hundred people listening to him make his single snare drum sing like an orchestra. Sam once told me that he could make more money in one day on Wall Street than he had ever made playing the clubs. But that was before he started playing with Zone and The Dangers.

I had never actually been to The Frontier. The space inside was tremendous. The entire three or four floors had been gutted, up and down, front and back, except for a little piece of the second floor, which hung precariously out into the room as a stage. The rest of the interior was a combination of pipes, exposed brick and cement floor. The people had all spent a lot of time and money trying to look like downtowners, but it didn't work. Pretty soon you'd be able to find The Frontier by the velvet ropes around the door and the limousines parked out in front.

I inched my way to the bar and squeezed in next to a group of yuppies who were arguing about Social Darwinism. They were all drinking something that was yellow and orange, and they were all drunk. I hate people who drink fancy-colored drinks. I decided to have a ginger ale.

There were three people working the bar: two girls and one guy. They were all busy and I waited patiently. Finally the guy came over to me and it wasn't until he was right in front of me that I realized that it was Kenny Adler. Kenny Adler and I went back a few years. He was once a bartender at a place called The Blue Bar. It was one of the first downtown bars for uptown people. He didn't like the way I drank and one night he threw me out. I'd been told that he had a wicked sense of humor, but I'd never seen it. Maybe we could have been friends if we didn't hate each other's guts.

"Oh, Kenny. For a minute I thought the bartenders here were going to be unfriendly."

"What do you want, Eddie?"

"Ginger ale on the rocks."

He sighed and put his hands up on the bar. "You can't mix here, Eddie. I'm sorry."

"I'm not mixing. I'm drinking ginger ale."

"Eddie, I'm serious."

"So am I."

"Look, Eddie. How'd you get in here anyway? This is supposed to be a classy joint."

I looked down the bar. Why couldn't I have gotten one of the women bartenders? A few seconds ago a ginger ale sounded fine. Now I wanted a scotch.

"Look, Kenny. Get me a fucking ginger ale before I climb over the bar and get it myself."

"Oh sure, Mr. Tough Guy. I heard about your friend Tony and about your little episode in the park with The Merk. What are you doing here? I thought they'd have you in jail by now."

"When was the last time someone told you to go fuck yourself?"

"Don't push me, Eddie," but he was already scooping ice into a glass.

One of the yuppies was trying very hard not to look at me. He had heard every word and didn't like the idea of standing next to someone who should have been in jail. I took my ginger ale from Kenny Adler and leaned my back against the bar and smiled at the yuppie. He ignored me. That was OK. At least he didn't try to talk to me.

Someone slapped me on the back and I turned to see Zone himself trying to get a drink from one of the women bartenders. Zone was a tall good-looking rock-and-roller with a good strong voice and a stage presence to put most downtown rockers to shame. Nobody knew what his real name was, or if he even had one. Ever since he'd been on the music scene his name was Zone, even before Zone and The Dangers. He was a competent musician, but it was his charisma and his ambition that made him so successful. I never had much to say to him. "How's it going, Zone?"

"Good, Eddie. Real good. We're working on a record deal and things look good. You know Buddy Feldman?"

"No."

"Yeah, he's managing us now, and getting us some gigs. He's got good sense and good connections. Giving us some direction, you know what I mean? Hey! You wanna come backstage?"

"Backstage" was actually a little room underneath the stage. Understage. There was nothing in it but a table and a lot of chairs. The only mirror I saw was being used as a chopping block for a large quantity of cocaine. The other members of the band, collectively The Dangers, were all there with a group of young girls with big eyes and open mouths. Sam was off in a corner listening to his Walkman and drumming lightly on the back of a chair.

I waved to the other Dangers, and Zone introduced me to Buddy Feldman who had his hand on some sixteen-year-old's leg. He took his nose away from the mirror long enough to ask, "You play?" My negative response terminated my existence as far as he was concerned, and he went back to his coke and his sixteen-year-old. Zone offered me some coke but didn't push me. He knew I was there to see Sam.

Sam didn't see me until I sat down in front of him. If Zone was making it on his stage presence, Sam was making it in spite of his. Sam was short and lanky. He had a big mouth that stretched almost from ear to ear and made him look a little bit like a frog. He turned off his Walkman and smiled. Or at least he opened his mouth, which was as close to a smile as he could get since his lips couldn't go back any further.

"Eddie, what's going on?"

"How's it going, Sam?"

"Good." He nodded toward the rest of the group. "We're doing real good."

"So I heard. You hear about Tony?"

His mouth closed. "Yeah, Eddie, I heard."

"Sam, I want to find out who killed him."

He took the earphones from around his neck and slowly wound the cord around them. Then he took the cassette out of the Walkman and put it in a case. He showed me the case. Dexter Gordon. He was probably the only one in the group who listened to jazz.

"Why don't you leave it for the cops?"

"The cops aren't going to do anything."

"It's asking for trouble, Eddie."

"How do you know?"

"Believe me."

"You know who killed him?"

"No. But I do know what kind of shit Tony was involved in."

"Like what?"

Sam started playing casually on the back of the chair. Sam and Tony had been close since the day they met down on Wall Street. Sam would keep secrets for Tony, but now Tony was dead, and all of the secrets in the world couldn't help him. Sam looked at the band gathered around the mirror. Maybe he was thinking what I was thinking. Maybe not. "We're going on in a few minutes, Eddie. Why don't you and I have a drink after the show?"

"OK, Sam."

I stood at the bar and had another ginger ale and watched Zone and The Dangers. I had heard them before, but each time I listened to them they were better. Too many bands forgot how important it was to rehearse. Zone and The Dangers were well rehearsed and they played clear, crisp rock-and-roll. Sam's drumming was lively and energetic, and it kept the whole place dancing.

After the show Sam and I sat at the bar, and we talked about the show and about Zone and The Dangers and Buddy Feldman. I let Sam talk as much as he wanted, and after he finished his first beer and me a ginger ale, we ordered another round. I think Kenny was ignoring us, but one of the female bartenders served us. Then I asked Sam again about Tony.

He looked up and down the bar. "You know who The Merk is, right?"

"Was," I corrected him.

He nodded. "Tony was working for The Merk."

"Doing what?"

"Well, I'm not sure. You see, The Merk was the agent for this guy Gus Harper."

"Yeah, I've heard that. Who the hell is Gus Harper?"

"I'm getting to that. Gus Harper controls all of the drugs on Avenue B. The cops know that. But they don't know who he is or how he operates."

"And you do?"

"Eddie, I'm going to tell you what I know about this, but let me tell you something first. I've figured all of this out on my own. Nobody told me this. I figured it out from what Tony's told me and from what I overhear."

"Overhear?"

He smiled, or opened his mouth, and put his Walkman on and started drumming lightly on the bar. The bartenders looked over with mild disinterest. Sam slipped the earphones off and handed them to me. I put them on and listened—to nothing.

I signaled Sam to turn the volume up. His mouth stayed open. "You'd be amazed what I hear that way," he said.

I handed the earphones back to him. "Nice trick, Sam."

He wrapped the Walkman up and took another sip of beer. "What I was trying to tell you is that nobody knows that I know what I know, and I want to keep it that way.

There's a guy named Wolfe. That's probably not his real name, but that's what they all call him. People say he's a banker or something. He's loaded. On Harper's instructions, Wolfe delivers the money, up front, to the suppliers.''

"Who are the suppliers?"

"I don't know. The thing is, nobody delivers drug money up front. We're talking millions of dollars. So Wolfe delivers the money to the suppliers."

"And Wolfe runs the stores?"

"The Merk ran the stores. He was in charge of the operations; you know, all the guys on the streets. Very neat. Very clean."

"Who's taken The Merk's place?"

"I don't know."

"How does Tony fit into all of this?"

"Well, this part is pretty interesting." And he lowered his voice appropriately, not that anybody was listening, or could have heard over the noise if they were. "Tony was working for The Merk. I don't know what he was doing, but he told me he was working for The Merk."

"What was he doing?"

"I don't know, but they were up to something. Tony would meet The Merk at special times and places. They were both scared of being followed when they met. I don't know, Eddie, but if you ask me, it sounds like The Merk was trying to pull a quick one on Gus Harper or something like that."

"You think Gus Harper found out about it and killed Tony and The Merk?"

"Could be."

"You know Tony was loaded when he was killed?"

Sam nodded. "I'm not surprised."

"You think he got his money from The Merk?"

"I have no doubt about that."

"Sam, you know anything about the Chinese?"

"What Chinese?"

"I don't know. The Merk said that the Chinese killed Tony."

Sam shook his head.

"You know about his family?"

"What about them? His fucking brother stole his girl friend."

I laughed. "I know, I went to the funeral."

"Tony was pretty ripped up about that, you know."

"Was he?"

"Yeah, I think so."

"Sam, one night I saw The Merk get picked up in a long black limousine. Whose car would that have been?"

"Wolfe's, probably. But let me tell you something about these people, Eddie. These people are big. They're not about to let somebody like you intrude on their business. They'll kill you faster than you can say 'scotch on the rocks.' "

"How about 'ginger ale'?"

"Eddie, I'm serious."

But I was already planning my next move.

Chapter 9

The Merk might have been dead, but the limousine was still in business. We picked it up on the corner of Avenue B and Fifth Street and followed it up the FDR Drive. I sat in the back of a taxicab and watched the colored lights of the bridges to Brooklyn and Queens bounce off the dark murky waters of the East River. The windows were open and a strong wind was coming in, and I felt cool for the first time since I'd stepped out of Gloria's air-conditioned Mustang. The smell of the East River was almost pleasant, and something about the speed of the taxi and the closeness of the water gave me that same feeling of nervous excitement that I used to get back in the old days when my friends and I would pile into my old El Camino and race down to the Keys for a weekend of fishing and drinking.

We turned off the highway at Fifty-ninth Street, and I leaned back in my seat and stretched my legs out as we followed the limousine slowly across town, through the late-evening streets of the Upper East Side.

New York is a city of different worlds. I was only ten minutes from the New York that I knew, but here the streets and the sidewalks were smooth, unbroken stretches of pavement joined neatly by the perfectly squared curbing. Cars parked along the curbs in even rows up and down the streets like well-behaved children in line for school. Everything was clean: the streets, the sidewalks, the buildings, even the garbage pails that sat neatly behind freshly painted iron railings.

In this world, everything worked and nothing was brutal. The elevators worked. Muggers and killers were captured and sent to jail. Drugs were purchased in penthouse apartments, not on dark seedy corners, and they were snorted with hundred-dollar bills from clean glass tables and chased with expensive champagne.

We drove across town, past all-night parking garages, movie theaters with long lines and well-dressed couples walking leisurely on the big open sidewalks. We turned uptown on Madison Avenue and drove past well-lighted jewelry stores and restaurants with names that I couldn't pronounce. Then we turned across again toward Fifth Avenue and we finally turned downtown at Central Park. The limousine stopped in front of a large apartment building on Fifth Avenue.

I got out of the taxi across the street and stood in the shadows of Central Park. I could hear the leaves rustling in the trees above me, and somewhere off in the park, a bird was singing. It was so quiet that I could hear the click from the traffic light every time it changed.

The building across the street was a large and solid gray structure that ran the entire length of the block. The name of the building, The Emperor, was written in script on the awning that stretched out from the doorway to the very edge of Fifth Avenue. Like the streets and sidewalks, the walls of the building were clean and perfect, and they shot straight up about twenty stories to the upper floors, where greenery spilled over the sides. There was nothing cheap about this building, except for the skinny passenger who had stepped out of the long black car.

His suit was about three sizes too big and in the light from the building I could see that it didn't match his tie. He had a long skinny face and his eyes darted around in a nervous way. His hair was slicked back and shiny, and he carried an old battered briefcase that looked as if it predated the First World War. The doorman didn't seem to notice that this was a drug addict in his Halloween costume.

I approached the building slowly. Through the iron grill

work on the front doors I saw the skinny passenger get into the elevator. When the elevator door shut I opened the outer door and stepped into the foyer. The doorman was a big ape who probably used to be a lifeguard or a bouncer in his younger days. He hadn't quite settled in yet behind his desk when he saw me, and I positioned myself so that he would be between me and the elevator. He came back around from behind the desk and stopped so that the floor indicator appeared just over his left shoulder. It was one of those old bronze hands that moves in a semicircle. On first glance it was at number three.

The doorman was taller than I had thought, and he looked down at me and said, "Yes, sir? What can I do for you?" He would have used the same tone of voice to say, "What the fuck do you want?"

"Oh, yes, I'm here to see Peter Samuels."

"Who?"

"Peter Samuels. He's my uncle. You can tell him Ted is downstairs. He's expecting me."

"You got the wrong address, buddy. There's no Peter Samuels here."

The bronze hand crept to nine. If this elevator had been in the Empire State Building it would have taken three days to get to the top. "Oh, of course. He's staying with someone. Let's see, what was his name?"

Fourteen, and the doorman was starting to get suspicious. "Gus Harper! That's it. He's staying with Gus Harper."

Nothing changed in the doorman's face. "Look, buddy. There's no Peter Samuels here and there's no Gus Harper. Now, why don't you beat it?"

Penthouse!

I smiled at the doorman. "OK. Sorry to bother you."

When I was out of view of the doorway, I turned to make sure that the doorman wasn't following me. Then I sneaked back along the edge of the building until I was about three feet from the door, and I stayed there flat against the building. I waited a long time. Finally a taxi pulled up and the doorman came out to open the car door. I slipped in through the doorway and went right for the elevator when I saw a pair of legs and a newspaper inside: an elevator man. The doorman would be coming back in a matter of seconds. There was a big fire door to my left. I tried it and stepped into a large stairwell that smelled of paint and ammonia. The door closed behind me and I looked up into a never-ending stairwell. There was a good chance that the penthouse door would be locked, and it was nineteen flights of stairs to find out.

Nineteen long flights.

I had had a lot of practice climbing stairs in my own building, but I still wasn't prepared for nineteen flights. When I got to the top I sat down to catch my breath. It took forever. I tried to rationalize why I was sitting in a stairwell in some palace on the Upper East Side, but I had to face facts. I was there on a whim. Finally I got up and tried the door marked "PH" and, of course, it was locked. The stairs kept going so I followed them. Suddenly I was outside looking at the entire east side of Manhattan and the boroughs beyond.

It was a view for the rich: both overpowering and peaceful. New York sparkled and glowed as if it were a distant planet viewed through a telescope.

I turned to find out where I had been unloaded. The stairs had brought me out on the northeast corner of the building and when I stepped out from the shadows of the sheltered stairway I saw that a large portion of the roof was being used as a terrace. It had trees, an outdoor bar and a built-in swimming pool. I felt as if I were in somebody's backyard in Scarsdale. In the middle was part of an apartment with large sliding glass doors. From where I stood I could see an enormous sitting room. The light flowed out through the glass doors and cast shadows across the entire roof.

I climbed over a low stone wall and I was on the terrace. Then I moved up and hid behind a tree to study the room. A woman sat with her legs draped across a couch. I couldn't see her face, but her body was slim and well formed. She was probably about nineteen. She was drinking and smoking and staring at the ceiling. She was naked.

Staying in the shadows, I crawled over to the edge of the roof. Ten feet below was more outdoor space and I jumped down. There was less terrace on the lower floor, but more interior. Big picture windows stretched the entire length of the building. All of them were dark. I walked around the corner and came to another stretch of windows and terrace. Light came from some of the windows.

The first room was a library about the size of the public library in my hometown. There was nobody in it. The next room looked like a study or game room. Hunting trophies and maps hung from the walls, and there was a pool table and a Ping-Pong table set off in opposite corners. The skinny drug addict I'd seen getting out of the limo was sitting awkwardly in a chair. Sitting at a rolltop desk nearby was an older man with a lot more class, but not enough to be the owner of a penthouse apartment. He had a big round head, a jaw that protruded halfway across the room and a greasy-looking mustache that had touches of gray in it. He was smoking a little cigar and he looked as if he smelled of garlic.

The older man was reading some papers on the desk. Occasionally he'd pick up a pen and sign something. Finally he stood up and handed the papers to the drug addict, who took them and stuffed them into his battered briefcase. The drug addict then pulled out an envelope, and the older man grabbed it and stuck it in his jacket pocket.

That's when all of the terrace lights came on and I turned in time to see a man's figure with a large wrench in his hand, but not in time to do anything about it.

The end of the world was coming. Everyone was hanging around in the lobby of a large hotel. We were all making jokes and acting nervous because we were scared.

Every once in a while a voice would come over the loudspeakers and announce a few names. Those people would go into the elevators and disappear. I asked someone where Tony was and they said he was getting changed. I decided to get changed too and I went to the changing rooms. Tony was sitting in a room behind a soundproof glass wall. He was playing his guitar. His guitar changed into a needle and he was shooting up. The needle changed into a gun and he was aiming it at his chest. Then his face started getting old. I asked someone what was happening and they said he was getting changed.

Then someone started pulling my arm. "It's time to get changed, Mr. Margolis." I resisted. I didn't know how to change. They pulled me harder and I still resisted. I fell down and people were leaning over me.

"Must have hit him pretty hard," a voice said. It echoed. Must have hit him pretty hard. Must have hit him pretty hard.

Then the whole floor started to move. We were all going up. I felt cheated. It was the end of the world and I hadn't even changed yet. We kept going up. Murphy was there and Holly was there. Murphy said, "I thought you'd want the young lady to be here."

Holly smiled and we embraced. "I haven't changed," I said.

The floor stopped moving and we were at a large door marked "PH." We stepped out onto a roof with bleachers set up overlooking New York City and an usher took us to our seats. The people who had gone up in the elevators had all gotten the good seats. We got popcorn and waited to see the end of the world, trying to figure out if it would blow up, or just melt.

Then it started getting hot. It was going to melt. I shut my eyes because I didn't want to watch. "Margolis, open your eyes," Murphy said. The melting must have started already because his voice had changed. "C'mon, Margolis!" He started slapping me on the face.

I opened my eyes. Murphy was standing over me smoking a cigar. He had been changed completely. He had a greasy mustache and a huge jaw. Holly was sitting on a chair next to me wearing a blue silk robe that revealed her long slender arms and the tops of her breasts. But she had been changed too.

"Thank you for coming," I said.

Holly laughed. "He's delirious," she said.

"He'll come to," Murphy said. Then to me, "Margolis, get up. We want to talk to you."

"I haven't changed yet."

"What's he talking about?" Murphy asked. "C'mon, Margolis, get up."

I sat up and rubbed my eyes. I was in the study where the skinny drug addict and the older man had been talking. My head felt as if it had been put through a food processor.

"Water," I heard myself say.

"Pierre, get him some water," Holly said.

I looked around for Pierre. He was leaning against the big wooden doors of the room. He had been the one with the wrench. He smiled at me and left the room.

"You're Edward Margolis," the man said.

"So what?"

I studied my company more carefully. Murphy was the older man I had seen talking to the drug addict. He wasn't as old as I had thought: maybe in his fifties, and he didn't smell like garlic either.

Holly was the woman I had seen upstairs, and she, on the other hand, was not as young as I'd thought. She had the body of a nineteen-year-old, but she was more like thirty-five. Her face was pretty in a healthy, rich sort of way. She had frosty golden hair down to her shoulders and mint green eyes, which clashed with her bright red lipstick and blue robe. The only thing that gave away her age were a few lines around her eyes and on her forehead, but she wore them well. She would have been exquisite if you were color-blind.

She was smiling at me. "You have a Florida driver's license, Mr. Margolis."

"So what?"

"One of my guards knocked you out sneaking around on my terrace. Pierre hates people from Florida."

"We'll have to take him to Miami sometime."

She laughed. "Except nobody in Miami is from Florida. They're all from New York."

I tried to smile, but my head hurt too much.

The man broke in, "Mr. Margolis, I'm afraid I'm going to have to ask you what you were doing out on the terrace."

"Don't be afraid. Go ahead and ask."

The woman laughed again.

"Mr. Margolis," the man continued. "You're not in a position to get smart with me."

"Who is this guy?" I asked the woman.

"That's Walter Scott. He's my attorney."

"Is he always such a bore?"

His face flushed with anger. "Look pal, we can have Pierre give you another bump to match the one you've got already."

Pierre took his cue and showed up with a silver tray with water and glasses. He was still smiling. He set the tray down in front of me and poured me a glass of water. I drank half of it and felt a little bit better. "Thank you, Pierre."

"You're welcome, sir." He resumed his position by the door.

"So, Mr. Scott here is your attorney. Pierre fetches water and hits people over the head with wrenches. Who are you?"

"You don't have to answer that," Walter Scott said.

"Don't mind him," she said to me. "My name is Nadine. Nadine Wolfe."

"Nadine!" Walter Scott raised his voice. "You're going to have to let me handle this my way. Now, Mr. Margolis, you have been caught in the act of breaking and entering, trespassing, invasion of privacy and several other felonious crimes for which we can have you prosecuted. Now for the last time, I ask you what you were doing out on the terrace.''

"I was spying."

"Spying on me?"

"No, not on you. On the skinny little drug addict you were talking to.''

Walter's eyes sank into the back of his head. Then he started to pace as if he were about to cross-examine me in court. "You admit you were spying?"

"Walter, darling, he just said that. Of course . . .''

"Nadine! Please let me handle this. Who do you work for?''

"Nobody. I'm unemployed."

"Ah, don't give me that crap! You're with the IRS, aren't you?''

"Well, if you must know, I'm with the EPA. I was checking the pool for toxic wastes.''

He stopped in front of me and stuck a finger in my face. "Listen, Margolis. I'm not going to take any more shit from you. Now start talking or I'll have Pierre start knocking your teeth out like Chiclets. You understand?''

"He's really got a temper, hasn't he?" I asked Nadine.

"I apologize for my attorney's behavior.''

"Apologize for my behavior! Nadine, I can't believe you. I suggest that we turn this matter over to the police immediately.''

I stood up. "I couldn't agree with you more, Mr. Scott. Nadine, where's the telephone? Pierre, bring me a telephone.''

"Oh, sit down, both of you!" Nadine was grinning from ear to ear. "You two are both impossible.''

I sat down, but Walter kept pacing.

"Walter, sit down, darling, please, you're making me nervous.''

Walter sat down in the corner, staring out the window. He was fuming.

Nadine was studying me. "Can I call you Edward?"

"Eddie."

"Eddie, why were you spying on us?"

"I told you. I wasn't spying on you. I was spying on that skinny drug addict you were entertaining."

"What makes you think he was a drug addict?"

"It's obvious."

"And why were you spying on him?"

"He was riding around in a limousine that was used by someone I saw at the scene of a crime, a murder. The victim was a friend of mine, and I'm looking for the murderer. Now I'd like to ask you a few questions."

"Wait, wait. I'm not finished yet," but she was smiling again. "What was your friend's name?"

"Tony Santucci."

She exchanged a glance with Walter Scott. "And who is it you saw in the limousine?"

"A punk called The Merk. He's dead too."

"You saw The Merk at the scene of your friend's murder?"

"That's right."

"Well, then, wouldn't it make sense that The Merk was the murderer?"

"No."

"Why not?"

"Because The Merk is dead too."

"And what was it you were hoping to accomplish by spying on this drug addict, as you call him?"

"I'm looking for Gus Harper." She started to look at Walter Scott again, but she stopped herself. "I have some information for him."

She stood up. "Walter, I'd like to talk to Mr. Margolis alone. Do you mind? Let me see you to the door. Pierre, will you please watch Mr. Margolis and make sure that he doesn't . . . get into any trouble?"

She and Walter left through the big wooden doors, and Pierre stood there and smiled at me. Behind the doors I could hear Nadine and Walter Scott arguing, but I couldn't understand what they were saying.

"What's going to happen to me, Pierre?"

"I don't know, sir."

"No ideas?"

"No, sir."

The door started to open and Nadine's arm came into view.

"Well, let me know, Pierre," I said, "if you get any ideas."

Nadine came in and held the door open. "Pierre, will you wait outside, please?"

"Yes, ma'am." And he left, with the door closing behind him.

"Interesting company you keep," I said.

"You have to get used to Walter. He's all right. What about you?"

"What about me?"

She sat down next to me on the couch. "Did you see me naked upstairs before?"

"Yup."

She smiled. "What did you think?"

"I thought you were nineteen."

"Hah! But thank you." She moved a little bit closer to me on the couch. I could smell her and she smelled good. "You wanted to ask me some questions, didn't you?"

"Yeah, how'd you get all this money?"

"I'm a widow. That's how I got all this money."

"Your husband was a banker, wasn't he?"

"My husband owned a controlling share of the First Star Savings Bank. You're too young to remember it. It was bought out in the seventies."

"Do you know who killed my friend?"

"No. I don't even know who he was."

"How about The Merk?"

"Nope."

"But Gus Harper you know."

"You said you had some information for him. Tell me, and I will have it relayed to him."

I stood up. "No, sorry. I have to talk to Mr. Harper directly."

"Sit down."

"Is that an order?"

"Does it have to be?" She could say that line the way only someone with a lot of money could. "You want to see Gus Harper, don't you?" she asked.

"Yes."

"OK, I can arrange it. We'll go see him tomorrow. He's in Southampton." She was smiling again, as if it were all a big joke.

I sat back down on the couch. It sounded fine, but something was wrong and it had something to do with Pierre on the other side of the door. "What if I don't want to go to Southampton?"

"You want to see Gus Harper, don't you?"

"Yes."

She leaned a little bit closer. "We'll drive out tomorrow in my car. You can stay here tonight. Besides, there's something else I want to talk to you about."

"What's that?"

"I need your help."

"My help?"

"You said before that you were unemployed."

"So what?"

"So I want to hire you."

"What for?"

"You seem to be pretty good at sneaking around. I think Walter is cheating me."

"Cheating you how?"

"I don't know. I think he's ripping me off."

"So fire him. What do you want me to do?"

"Hang around for a while. We'll go out to Gus's tomorrow. Why don't you see what you can get out of Walter?"

"What can I possibly do? 'Hey, Walter, is it true you're ripping off Nadine?' "

"I'm sure you can think of a more subtle approach."

"I think you could probably think of a more subtle approach yourself. I'm a prisoner here, aren't I?"

"Eddie, you're not a prisoner. It's just that I want you

to hang around for a while. Understand? Would you take a walk with me on the terrace?''

''Is Pierre going to come with his wrench?''

''No. Just you and me.''

''OK.''

We took a private elevator to the upper floor and we walked through the room where I had seen her before. She led me out onto the terrace and we walked around under the trees. We didn't talk much. Then we sat on an outdoor love seat overlooking the park. Everything was peaceful and quiet except for the alarms ringing inside my head.

Chapter 10

I sat between Nadine and Walter Scott in the back of Nadine's Rolls-Royce and watched our chauffeur through the soundproof glass as he talked to the guard at the gate house. They could have been planning a revolution against the upper classes for all we could have heard. Nadine grew impatient and leaned forward to push aside the glass between us and the front seat. "Matthew, what the hell is going on up there?"

"I'm sorry, Mrs. Wolfe," he answered, meeting her eyes in the rearview mirror. "He says he has strict instructions not to allow anyone in except you and Mr. Scott."

"Well, what's the problem?"

I was the problem and we all knew it.

"Oh, shit," she said and she pushed the button on her door. The window rolled down silently and the car filled up with the warm salty air of the Hamptons. The guard bent over slightly to show his face, but not so much so as to appear to be looking inside the car. It was an elegant position that probably took years of practice.

"I'm sorry, ma'am. Mr. Harper's instructions."

"Yeah, well, Mr. Harper is an asshole. Let me talk to him." She climbed out of the car, a flurry of angry arms and legs in a bright yellow dress, and she followed the guard into the gate house.

Walter Scott let out a long drawn-out sigh and sat gazing out of the window. I listened to the crickets chirping in the early-afternoon sun. The guard came out of the gate house and stood, looking embarrassed.

Finally Nadine stormed out of the gate house. Her face was flushed red and it clashed with her bright yellow dress. "Go talk to your boss!" she screamed at the guard, and she got back into the car with a slam of the door and the triumphant closing of the window. So much for the crickets. The guard disappeared into the gate house, and seconds later the iron gates swung back and we proceeded slowly up a pebbled driveway shaded by large pine trees.

The driveway took a series of acute turns, and suddenly the trees gave way to a rolling lawn and a stone mansion. It was big, but not bigger than Yankee Stadium. A servant met us by the front door of the mansion. He looked like a parody of John Wayne. He said something to our chauffeur and we drove on past the house, past a large greenhouse, a swimming pool and into more woods. Finally we arrived in a circular parking area behind a comparatively modest wooden beach house. It was painted white, but flowers colored all of the windowsills—an odd assortment of colors that reminded me of Nadine.

Matthew opened the door for us and I followed Nadine and Walter Scott around a little walkway to the front of the house. Suddenly a strong warm wind welcomed us, and a long strip of ocean and beach came into view. A long flight of wooden steps led down to the beach and a small flight led up to a patio attached to the house.

Gus Harper stood at the top of the steps on the patio. He was tall and broad-shouldered, and he had a long face with teeth that glistened in the sun. He hadn't shaved and the whiskers from his beard were an interesting mix of gray and blond. His hair was mostly gray and he wore it a little bit longer than one would have expected. He wore a pair of khaki shorts that showed a pair of good strong legs and a plain white T-shirt that emphasized his tan. He looked good, but I guess it's easy to look good when you have millions of dollars and you live by the beach.

Nadine walked past him and flopped down on one of the beach chairs on the patio. Walter Scott shook his hand and sat next to Nadine. That left me. I felt his eyes burning through me and I froze two steps from the patio. He would have stood like that all day. I climbed the last two steps and extended my hand. "Eddie Margolis."

We shook hands. "Gus Harper. Have a seat."

A servant appeared from within the house and made drinks for us. Gus Harper and Nadine had gin and tonics. Walter Scott drank beer. I had a ginger ale. The servant went back inside the house, and we all sat there sipping our drinks and saying nothing.

I was out of New York City and I wasn't in Newark, New Jersey. I looked out over the beach and the waves and tried not to think about my dubious status as a guest of Gus Harper. The ocean was wild, and it pounded the beach with its white foam and sprinkled the air with fine spray. I was content to sit and watch the seagulls soaring over the surf, bobbing up and down with the wind and singing in their high-pitched voices. Why did people live in New York? What could New York possibly offer that was better than the sun, the wind and the open sea?

Nature had just about subdued me into a euphoric state of mind when Nadine's voice cracked the silence. "I want an apology, Gus."

"You don't deserve one."

"I do deserve one. You're a pompous asshole."

"Oh, stop it, Nadine! You messed up and you know it. Now let's stop the name-calling and figure this out."

"Not until I get an apology."

"For Christ's sake, Nadine! Grow up!"

"I am grown up."

"How did he find you?"

"I don't know. Ask him. He was sneaking around the terrace and Pierre hit him with a wrench."

"And I have a bump on my head to prove it," I said.

Gus Harper turned to me. "What were you doing up on the terrace?"

"Like I told Nadine and Walter here, I was spying on a drug addict who came in a limousine."

"And you followed him to Nadine's apartment?"

"That's where he ended up."

"Shit. Nadine, where the hell did you find that guy?"

"He was the new one. After The Mer—"

"Jesus. Nadine, sometimes I think you got your head up your ass."

"Oh, fuck you, Gus! All you do is sit around and criticize. Let's see you get out there and do something."

"Excuse me," I said, but nobody listened.

Gus roared on. "Great. You let the guy come to your apartment?"

"How was I supposed to stop him?"

"Excuse me!" I tried again.

"You tell him! That's how!" Gus was shouting. "Jesus H. fucking Christ, Nadine! You fucking tell him!"

I couldn't take it anymore. I stood up and dropped my glass on the tiled patio and it shattered. "Excuse me!"

"Sit down!" Gus Harper yelled.

That did it. I started walking down the steps.

"Sit down, goddamn it!" he yelled after me.

I ignored him and I walked around to the back of the house. The car was gone so I followed the driveway back toward the main house. I didn't know what I was going to do, but I didn't care. If I was a prisoner, they'd have to treat me like a prisoner. If I was a guest, I'd come back some other time, when the mood was better.

Why did I care who killed Tony? He was dead already. And while I was at it, how had I let some two-bit whore talk me into giving up booze? Booze at least had kept me out of trouble. The first thing I'd do when I got back to New York would be to have a drink in Tony's memory at The Pit.

Then I heard the dogs.

It wasn't the casual bark of a couple of dogs enjoying a weekend in the Hamptons. They were calling my name, and I didn't like the way it sounded. They weren't a hundred yards away when I spotted them: two German shepherds coming at me from the main house as if I had just stolen their dinner. Or as if I were their dinner.

There was no running away. They'd be on top of me before I made it halfway back to the beach house. I could freeze but they didn't look as if they'd care. They didn't look as if they'd care if I were the founder of the ASPCA. They were fifty yards away and I was starting to shake at the menace in their voices.

I looked around for something to defend myself with—a stick or rock or something—but there was nothing but grass and trees. When they were about twenty-five yards away I made a dash for the nearest tree. I leaped at it with both hands and legs and shimmied my way up the trunk. Then I grabbed a branch and pulled myself up. Their hungry jaws attacked the trunk just as my feet were out of reach. They leaped at the trunk and for an instant I thought they were going to climb the tree. Their teeth snapped just inches below the limb I sat on, so close that I could smell the rotten heat of their breath.

After a few futile leaps they just stood there and barked. I caught my breath and then climbed up to a higher branch so I could sit and dangle my legs without fear of losing a foot. There was nothing to do but wait until someone came to my rescue.

Finally I saw two servants approaching from the main house. The one who looked like John Wayne carried a couple of chains and leashes. The other one was taller and carried a rifle. They didn't say anything as they approached the tree. John Wayne patted the dogs on the head and slipped a collar and a leash on each of them. They stopped barking immediately. He pulled them back from the tree and looked up at me. He had a funny smile on his face, which told me that he knew how much he looked like John Wayne. "It's all right," he said. "They won't hurt you. You can come down now."

I climbed down to the lower branch and then let myself drop to the ground. That instigated a new round of vicious growls from the dogs and they pulled on their leashes to get at me. I prayed that he had John Wayne's strength, as well as his looks.

Walter Scott came up behind me. "OK, Mr. Margolis. They won't hurt you. Let's go have a chat. Lead the way, fellas."

The two servants started off with the dogs back toward the main house. I dusted myself off and inspected a few scratches on my arms.

"Had a little scare, did you?" Walter Scott said, chuckling to himself.

"Oh, it was nothing. I just wanted to see if they could climb trees."

"You like to talk tough, don't you, Mr. Margolis?"

"I am tough."

"Maybe. But you're stupid. What made you think Harper was just going to let you leave?"

"Why shouldn't he?"

"Why should he?"

"Why, is he hiding something?"

"We're all hiding something, Mr. Margolis." We started to walk back to the main house.

"What are you hiding, Walter?"

"If I told you what I was hiding, then it wouldn't be hidden anymore, would it?"

"Yeah, but maybe I already know what it is."

"Mr. Margolis, what exactly did you see last night when you were out on the terrace?"

"What is it you're trying to hide, Walter? The papers you signed or the envelope you stuck in your pocket?"

"Both can be easily explained."

"Don't bother. I don't care."

"But I do, Mr. Margolis. You see, as Nadine's attorney, it is my duty to look out for her better interests. The documents I signed related to the estate of her husband. I have a power of attorney from her and I signed them on her behalf. There's no secret about that. The envelope contained certain documents that belonged to her husband but fell into the wrong hands. They were being handed to me to hold in escrow pending the settlement of the estate.''

"So what's the secret?"

"The documents were of an extremely sensitive nature. They were, let us say, potentially dangerous to the reputation of the deceased. I have obtained them upon special understanding with opposing counsel. Nadine does not know of their existence, and it would be better if she remained ignorant of the matter.''

"For your sake?"

"No, for hers. The documents contained evidence of certain . . . indiscretions, of which Nadine was not aware. If she were to find out about them now, it would cause her useless emotional distress.''

"What you're saying then is that you don't want me to tell Nadine that you took an envelope from the drug addict who came to see you last night.''

"It's not what I want. It's what I believe to be in Nadine's better interests.''

"And who was the drug addict?"

"He was an assistant to one of the attorneys we are dealing with.''

I laughed at him. "He was a goddamned drug addict.''

"I am not concerned with the weaknesses of my adversary's assistants.''

"Do you always conduct business in the middle of the night?''

"When I have to.''

We were at the main house. The dogs were led off to a kennel that I hadn't seen when we drove past the house. The servant with the rifle led us into the house by a side door and we entered a small sitting room with no windows. The servant left us, and Walter Scott made himself a drink and I sat on the couch and watched him.

He faced me with a drink in his hand and looked casually around the room. "I told them that I would see that you were taken to the main house unharmed. I have done that. Our little chat never occurred. Harper will probably be down to see you soon. In the meantime, Mr.

Margolis, I suggest that you contemplate your position here. You have nothing to gain, and everything to lose.''

"Were they pictures, Walter?"

"I'm sorry?"

"The documents. Were they pictures?"

"I told you, Mr. Margolis. Our little chat never occurred." He turned and walked out, and the thud of the door echoed in the little room.

Chapter 11

I sat there for a long time. Then I got up and walked around the room. It was sparsely furnished with a tiled floor and large modern paintings on the walls. The paintings were white canvases with splotches of yellow and red thrown on them. They didn't mean anything to me so I sat back down on the couch. Nobody came in and nothing happened, and after a while I stretched out and went to sleep.

When I woke up everything in the room was exactly the same. I felt as if I had been asleep for a long time, but there were no windows and I couldn't tell if it had gotten dark out. I felt a compelling need to know the time and I got up to find someone.

The door was locked.

It's funny how the mind works. However long I had been in that room was long enough to contemplate its entire contents. And yet it was not until the instant that I felt the lock on the door that I realized I was sitting in a room with a fully stocked bar.

I leaned against the door and breathed deeply. I was nervous as hell. Not about the door being locked, but about the bar being unlocked. I tried desperately to think of a reason not to have a drink, but my mind drew a blank. I was in trouble.

I stood leaning against the door, afraid to move. If I left the door I would go to the bar. There was nowhere else to go. Where else could I go? Back to the couch? What would I do on the couch? There was no place to go but to the bar. I tried the door again. Then I pounded on it with my fists. "Hey! Let me out of here!"

I was answered by silence.

"Let me out of here!"

More silence.

OK. I would go to the couch and go back to sleep. I walked slowly past the bar and to the couch. I felt like the groom at a shotgun wedding. I lay down and closed my eyes. They bounced back open. I closed them again. They opened again.

This wasn't going to work. Rationally, I had two choices. I could give in or I could fight it. If I gave in, I would have one drink. What was wrong with one drink? If I fought it, it would be a long constant battle and I had no idea how long it would go on. It could be all night before someone came in to see me. I deserved a drink.

I got up and walked to the bar,.thinking that there had to be a way to stop myself. I opened the cabinet. There was Chivas Regal and two bottles of unblended scotch. There were glasses and there was ice. There was a bottle of Johnnie Walker Red. I was really in trouble.

Then I heard the door open behind me. A servant came in with a tray of food. It was a servant I had not seen before. He put the tray down on the table near the couch.

"What time is it?" I asked.

He looked at his watch. "It's almost eight o'clock, sir." He saw me looking at the bar. "Can I fix you a drink?"

"Does it lock?"

"Sir?"

"Can you lock this up? I can't take the temptation."

He laughed "Oh, no need to resist, sir. It's there to drink."

"No, I'm serious. I don't want to drink. Can you lock it?"

He looked upset. "Well, I suppose if . ."

"Please. I'd appreciate it."

I left the bar and sat down in front of the food: a colorful array of salad and pasta, and a bottle of wine. He locked the bar and then stood in front of me. "Will there be anything else, sir?"

"Here, take this." I held out the bottle of wine.

He started to laugh but then saw that I was serious. He took the bottle and left.

After dinner the servant came back in with a tray of coffee, followed by Gus Harper, who had changed from his beach clothes to a pair of casual pants and a light blue sweater. There was some commotion as the servant poured coffee and picked up my dinner tray, and then Gus Harper and I sat alone in the room with our coffee. He sat in a big armchair and rested one ankle on the other knee.

"May I call you Eddie?"

"Please."

"Eddie, I'm sorry to have kept you like this, but you understand I couldn't very well let you wander off until I knew more about you."

We sipped our coffee. Mine was too hot and I put it back down.

"What do you want to know?"

"Well, let me tell you what I've found out about you and you can fill in the blanks."

"Or correct you if you're wrong."

"I'm never wrong."

"You were wrong about The Merk."

"We'll get to that." He sipped his coffee. Either his was cooler than mine, or he had no nerves in his mouth. "Your name is Edward Margolis. You're from Homestead, Florida, originally and you have a father who still lives there."

"Wrong already. He lives in the Keys now."

"You live on Christie Street in the city. You have no job and you're an alcoholic."

"Was an alcoholic."

"Once an alcoholic, always an alcoholic. You asked my servant to lock up the bar and you made him take away the wine, one of the Sonoma Valley's finest, incidentally. Oh, how was your dinner?"

"Fine, thanks."

"I stole the chef from one of my favorite restaurants. Anyway, you still don't trust yourself with booze around."

"So what?"

"So you're an alcoholic. You were friendly with Tony Santucci who was killed a few weeks ago in his apartment. You were questioned by the police. You were also in the park when The Merk was shot. Again you were questioned by the police. You have taken it upon yourself to track down the person who killed your friend Tony. How am I doing?"

"Not bad."

"You followed a limousine formerly used by The Merk and somehow got past the doorman and the elevator man and ended up on Nadine's terrace."

"Want to know how?"

"Yes, eventually, but not now. You followed the limousine in hopes that it would lead you to me, which it did. You claim you have certain information for me. Now what have I missed?"

"I once caught a ten-pound grouper on six-pound test line and I landed him without a net. I cooked him with carrots and lemon, and he was delicious. I think I went to bed early that night."

He smiled and showed his sparkling white teeth. "What I don't understand, Eddie, is what you plan to do once you find your friend's murderer."

I picked up my coffee and tried it. Much better. "I don't know. I haven't gotten that far yet."

"What if I killed Tony Santucci?"

"Then I would have gotten that far."

"I can't decide," he said, picking up his coffee, "whether you're reckless or just plain stupid."

"Both. Did you know that The Merk was trying to pull a fast one on you?"

His eyes became suddenly serious, but he managed to take a sip of coffee. His reaction could have meant one of three things. First, he could have known that The Merk was pulling something, and he was surprised that I knew it also. Second, he could have suspected that The Merk was up to something and now wanted to hear what I had to say. Or lastly, it was possible that he had never thought about The Merk, but now that I had mentioned it, it made perfect sense to him.

What he said was, "I have no doubt that The Merk would never have tried such a thing."

"Is that why you had him killed?"

He put his coffee down and leaned back with his hands behind his head. "I did not have The Merk killed. I did not have anybody killed. I'm not a killer, Eddie."

"What do you do when someone double-crosses you?"

"What do you do?"

"I don't have anything to lose."

"That, Eddie, is where your thinking leads you astray. A killer is a killer by heart. Someone born with the heart of a killer will kill as quickly over an insult as he will over a billion dollars. Someone like you or me couldn't kill if it meant saving the entire western world. Once a killer, always a killer. It's like being an alcoholic."

"It's hard to believe that someone like you can function in this line of work without knocking off people who are uncooperative."

"It's not easy, I'll admit. Let's take you for instance. If I were a killer, I'd have you killed. The fact that you got up to Nadine's and knew who I was would have been enough to have you killed. But now you're a problem. I haven't decided yet what to do with you. I suppose that once I'm convinced that your only real interest is finding out who killed your friend, I'll let you go. You see, I'm really rather invulnerable."

"Or so you think."

"No, I am. When I was younger, in college, I decided that the only reason you had to work was because society told you to work. There are thousands of ways to make money without working, but you have to be smart enough to recognize that. Only the stupid work for a living. But there was something else. There were two things that I knew I never wanted to do. I never wanted to be responsible for another man's death. And I never wanted to go to jail. And based on what I knew, and what I knew I didn't want, I have built this." He gestured at our surroundings.

"You really think the police will never get you?"

"If they try to get me, I'll know about it and they'll find a nice house with nobody home."

"And what will you do?"

"Start over."

"Just like that?"

"Just like that."

"You sound as if you've thought about this before."

"My life is built around it."

"And what about The Merk?"

"What about him?"

"He was a killer by heart."

"I can't be responsible for the actions of others."

"He worked for you."

"But he never killed on my orders."

"It seems like an arbitrary place to draw the line."

"Drawing a line anywhere is arbitrary."

"I'd say it's hypocritical."

"No, Eddie. It's never hypocritical to draw a line. It's only hypocritical to draw a line and then cross it."

"And you don't believe that The Merk was making a move against you?"

"No. But I'm interested in why you think he was."

"He was working with my friend."

He leaned forward in his seat and put his hands on his knees. "The Merk was working with Tony Santucci?"

"That's right."

"OK, I'm interested now. Talk to me."

I forced a laugh. "You haven't decided what you're going to do with me yet. Why should I tell you anything?"

He smiled. "I like you, Eddie. You may be full of shit, but even if you are, you know exactly what to say to get my interest. I'll tell you what I'll do. I don't know how much you know, but I'll tell you a few things that may help you. Then you can decide whether or not you want to talk to me. I think that's pretty fair. What do you say?"

"Sounds fair."

"Good. Now, do you know anything about your friend Tony's family?"

"I was at the funeral. I met them briefly."

"Tony's brother Frank Santucci imports drugs. I don't know where they come from, or who his connections are, and I, of course, am not going to disclose how I know this, but Frank Santucci smuggles heroin into the country."

He smiled when he saw my mouth open. If he had been trying to surprise me, he had succeeded. But I wasn't going to let him bask in the glory of his success. I moved on. "So that means that if Tony Santucci was working for The Merk, then your suppliers had infiltrated your camp."

He nodded his head. "Frank Santucci has been trying to usurp power for some time. He's a smart asshole, and they're the hardest to beat. A smart man who is a gentleman, is a pleasure, because he's a pleasant challenge. An asshole who is stupid is no problem because you can outtalk him. But a smart asshole is a tough cookie."

"Too bad his brother wasn't so tough."

"You haven't told me what you know about your friend and The Merk."

"I saw The Merk leaving Tony's building when I got there."

"I know."

"The Merk told me that the Chinese had killed Tony."

"Did he?"

"Do you use the Chinese as suppliers?"

"Eddie, it's no secret that the Chinese are the biggest importers of heroin in this country."

"I'd also heard rumors through the junkies downtown that Tony and The Merk were working together to pull a fast one on you."

He waited, and when I didn't say anything he said, "Well, what else?"

"That's it."

He smiled. "Are you making that up just so it looks as if you had some information for me?"

"No. I've heard it."

"But that's all you know?"

"That's it."

He laughed and shook his head. "OK. So maybe you got more out of me than I got out of you. But that's OK, because I have a feeling you're going to help me. You'll find out who killed your friend, and who killed The Merk."

"I still have a hard time believing you'll let me go."

"You can't do anything to me."

"I could turn you in for harboring dogs with a known vicious propensity."

He laughed. "You sound like Walter. I trained those dogs myself, Eddie. They have as much heart for killing as I do."

"It's too bad you can't train your employees like that."

"I think you'll agree that there's a big difference between dogs and humans."

"Not where I live."

He laughed again. "Well, in that case, I hope I never have to see where you live."

"There's one thing that still bothers me."

"What's that?"

"Well, let's just say that Frank Santucci learned about a certain Chinese supplier and proceeded to . . ."

"Cut off the supply?"

"Yeah, cut off the supply. Why would the Chinese go after Tony?"

"Who should they go after?"

"Frank Santucci."

"Eddie, you seem to forget that Tony had a last name."

"Yeah, but I doubt Tony would have been involved in any actual movement against the Chinese."

"He still had a last name."

"So you think the Chinese did it?"

He shrugged. "I don't point fingers."

"You think they killed The Merk too?"

He shrugged again.

"Do you think that Walter is cheating Nadine?"

He smiled. "Of course, he is. She knows he is and he knows she knows he is."

"So what does she want me to do?"

"Nothing. She just told you about that to keep you around."

"Is that so?"

"Well, don't be too flattered. She had a professional interest in bringing you out here."

"She ever have a professional interest in you, Gus?"

He laughed, but his heart wasn't in it. "I won't comment on that one, Eddie."

It was late when Gus left, and a servant led me up a massive stairway and down a few impressive hallways; he left me in front of a door with an obsequious nod.

Inside was a bedroom big enough to sleep an army. Nadine was on the bed wearing a pink nightgown that showed a lot of leg.

"Close the door," she whispered.

I closed the door and sat down on a big chair by the door.

"How was your talk with Gus?"

"It was a blast. What's up? I'm tired."

Her face broke into a devious smile. "Eddie. Why don't you stay up for a while with me and talk?"

"OK. Tell me about your husband."

"He's dead, I told you."

"How did he die?"

"In a car accident, about three years ago. He drove our Jaguar off a cliff, and it landed upside down in the ocean. I was with him."

"In the car?"

She pulled up her nightgown and showed me an impressive scar on her right leg that ran from the knee right up to the waist. "That's how I got this. The doctors said it was a miracle that I survived."

"Must have been quite a fall."

"We landed in one of the worst coves on the Pacific coast. My husband's body washed up on shore two weeks later almost fifty miles from the crash. Or, I should say, what was left of his body."

"What happened to his estate?"

"I got it."

"All of it?"

"All of it."

"Any problems?"

"What do you mean?"

"With the estate?"

"No. Walter handled it."

"Walter said that the drug addict was there to take care of some business regarding the estate. Any truth to that?"

"The estate closed over a year ago. I don't know of any business left. Besides, the drug addict works for Gus."

"So Walter was lying?"

"I guess so."

"He's cheating you, Nadine."

She pulled her nightgown back down but didn't say anything.

"He's cheating you. You didn't need me to tell you that he was cheating you. Why didn't you just handcuff me and throw me in the trunk of your Rolls-Royce?"

"Why all the questions, Eddie?"

"Tell me more about your husband."

"What about him?"

"How old was he?"

"Fifty-two."

"Was he faithful?"

"Faithful?" She started to laugh. "He was impotent."

"Are you sure?"

"Yes, I'm sure. So was every doctor money could buy."

"Must have been hard on you."

"I don't want to talk about it."

"Well, what do you want to talk about?"

"Nothing."

"Fine." I stood up. "It wasn't my idea to come in here in the first place."

Again, that devious smile. "You do have a way about you, don't you?"

"Are we finished?"

She laughed. "You're gonna need me one day, Eddie."

"Well, I'll see you then."

"You better hope so."

Chapter 12

When the summer heat locks in on New York, bad tempers grow like weeds in an abandoned lot. Rational adults suddenly become hot angry children who feel that their sweat and misery justify rash behavior. Fights break out over parking spaces and old ladies die of heat stroke, and nobody does anything because they're all just too damned hot to think about it. I stepped out of Penn Station onto Seventh Avenue expecting to be back in this hot steamy nightmare but instead found the city swept clean by a cool clear breeze coming off the Hudson River. The hot fuzzy edge that had somehow surrounded everything for the past few weeks had suddenly lifted, and the city was sharp and alive. I decided to walk home.

The east side of Seventh Avenue just below Thirty-fourth Street is junk-food row. I counted eight different fast-food places on one block, and that's not to mention the ones around the corner on Thirty-third Street. Macy's and Gimbel's and Penn Station pull pedestrians into the area by the thousands. The block immediately south of junk-food row always has one of the biggest taxi jams in the city. Taxis are three-deep at the curbs. The ones on the right try to cut left to get to the Statler Hotel. The ones on the left try to get to the right to get to Penn Station. Empty taxis are so hard to find that people will grab one in the middle of the street, holding up everyone behind them while they get in, pull their bags in and close the doors. From the sidewalk it's a rather comical sight as people drag their luggage or shopping bags into the middle of Seventh Avenue, only to become stranded in a sudden wave of oncoming traffic.

As I worked my way south down Seventh Avenue into the garment district, the taxis suddenly gave way to the double- and triple-parked trucks and workers pushing big rolls of fabrics on handcarts. Men stood in open doorways and on delivery platforms and on the backs of trucks, drinking beers and whistling at the girls who walked by. In the heat there would have been screaming matches over damaged goods and fights over crap games. But today everything was pleasant and even the bosses were out on the streets sharing beer with their employees and looking at the girls.

When I passed St. Vincent's hospital, twenty blocks down, I turned left down Greenwich Avenue and headed for the heart of the Village. Greenwich Village is the true melting pot of New York City. No single group of people can claim it. It belongs to the rich, to the poor, to the artists, to the con men, to the gays, to the hippies, to the druggies, to the yuppies, to the freaks, to the Italians, to the New Jersey teenagers, to the students, to the drunks and to anyone else who wants a part of it. On Sixth Avenue tourists sit in uncomfortable chairs while real live Village artists draw their portraits. The merchants line the streets selling anything from old Playboy magazines and used record collections to "handcrafted" African artifacts.

Bleecker Street was bustling with shoppers popping in and out of bakeries and record stores. On the corner of Bleecker and Thompson streets, a group of young black men was singing Motown love ballads. People from the street joined in, and it was impossible to tell who was performing and who was listening.

By the time I got to my neighborhood I was exhausted, and it was an unexpected surprise to find my elevator working. As I rode up to the seventh floor I realized that I had not been home in over two days.

There was a large envelope leaning against my door. I took it into my apartment and collapsed on the bed to open it. It was a catalog from Midnight Jewelers, a small but handsome pamphlet with neat colored photographs of earrings, hairpins, necklaces and bracelets. Everything had lots of colors and feathers, and I thought that Nadine would have loved the catalog if it weren't for the fact that it wasn't Tiffany's. There was a note to me scribbled on the back in childish handwriting:

Eddie,
Thought you'd like to see this. Call me sometime. I got a phone. 555-3050.

Love,
Holly

Somehow I had expected to recognize her handwriting, and I sat there and looked at it for a long time, trying to remember what she looked like and wondering if I had ever really known her. I picked up the phone and dialed her number. It rang about ten times and I hung up.

That night I went to New Jersey.

The front room of Sanka's had a long bar and lots of tables and a jukebox that played rock-and-roll from the 1950s. It was a lively fun crowd of neat, casually dressed hipsters from Hoboken and New York, and I felt a stinging pang of regret that I couldn't stand around and drink with them. It wasn't a small pang. It was a great big one, like the kind that a kid gets in a toy store when his mother tells him he can't have a toy.

The bartender told me that I could find Frank Santucci in the back, and by moving one foot in front of the other I managed to get away from the bar and into the back room. The back room would have been the place to buy booze in the days of Prohibition, or to gamble if it had been the right kind of crowd, but now it was just a place for people to sit in the dark. It cost five bucks to get into the back room and there was a small stage set up for a band, but nobody was playing yet. The back room was probably on New York City time, which meant the first band would not go on until around midnight.

Frank sat alone at a table with a bottle of scotch and an empty glass. His head was down on his folded arms, and I sat down at the table and looked at the small bald spot on the top of his head. A waitress came over and asked me if I wanted anything. I didn't. I said Frank's name a few times, but he didn't wake up. Then I picked up the scotch bottle and banged it down on the table. The thud was louder than I had expected and Frank jerked his head up in bewilderment.

The left side of his face was creased from where he had been lying on it, and his hair was messy and matted. His green eyes were bloodshot and he looked like hell. There was a familiar look to his face that bothered me. It was a face I had seen a thousand times and yet I could not place.

He cleared his throat and leaned back in his chair and looked at me.

"Eddie Margolis," I said. "I was a friend of your brother's."

"Yeah, that's right. Eddie." He picked up the bottle and poured about three shots' worth of scotch into his glass. "To my brother," he toasted and he downed the whole glass. It was impressive. I knew someone who used to be able to do that. And suddenly I knew why he looked so familiar. His was the drunken face I used to see in the mirror every morning.

He pushed the bottle toward me. "Have a drink."

I pushed it back.

"OK, don't have a drink. Sit there and stare at me." He poured another drink, getting a good half of it in his glass, but he didn't drink it. "That fucking friend of yours is a bitch, did you know that?"

"Who? Tony?"

"No, not fucking Tony. Fucking Gloria."

"Why is Gloria a bitch?"

He looked away from me and his eyes traveled around the room. He continued without looking at me. "Are you into this scene? This punk scene? You must know some of these people. They're all from New York." I turned in my seat to look around and I actually saw some familiar faces from my club days. From behind me Frank kept talking. "Man, I'm telling you. Some of the girls who come in here you just couldn't believe."

I turned to face him. "Why is Gloria a bitch?" I asked again.

His eyes focused on me briefly and for an instant I thought maybe he was sober, but he leaned over the table and grabbed my collar and then held on to it just so that he wouldn't fall backward. "Don't talk about her. You don't know her. You're not allowed to talk about her."

I didn't say anything.

"Do you understand that?"

I still didn't say anything. A man walked over to our table. "Everything all right, Frank?"

Frank let go of my collar and looked at him. He was a big man, probably about six foot four, and must have weighed over two hundred and fifty pounds. He looked as if he drank outboard-motor oil for kicks. He just stood there, looking at us.

"Yeah, everything's fine," Frank said. "Thanks, Lenny." And Lenny somehow managed to disappear into the crowd.

"Who was that?" I asked.

"That's Lenny. He looks out for me. What are you doing here anyway?"

"Frank, I want to find out who killed Tony."

"Why do you care?"

"I don't know. Maybe because nobody else does."

"That's for damned sure." And he polished off his drink.

"Frank, I need your help. Gus Harper says that . . ."

"Who's Gus Harper?"

"Oh, c'mon, Frank. I did my homework. Don't play stupid on me."

"Go ahead. I want to hear what Gus Harper said."

"He thinks the Chinese killed your brother."

"How do you know that?"

"He told me."

"He told you? Gus Harper told you?"

"Yeah, that's right."

And then he started to laugh. He laughed hard, and when he stopped he wiped his bloodshot eyes and poured another drink. Then he leaned forward on the table and said, "Get out of here."

"What's the matter, don't you believe me?"

"You don't understand. There is no Gus Harper."

"What do you mean?"

"I mean there is no Gus Harper. Here, have a drink."
He pushed the bottle toward me and I pushed it back.
"OK, I'll have one for you." He drank about half of what
was in his glass. He could sit and talk, but I figured he'd
have a hell of a time trying to walk.

"Frank, I talked to Gus Harper."

"Well, that's a nice trick. Maybe you smoke too much
dope, how do I know?" He stopped suddenly and nodded
toward the door. "Jesus. Look at that, would you?"

I turned and saw a couple of punked-out girls coming in
from the front room. One was tall and had purple frizzed-
out hair. The other had red hair and was medium height,
but she had a chest that would cause a riot in a men's
locker room. It was too dark to see their faces but nobody
would have looked at their faces anyway. They were both
wearing spotted skintight pants and high heels, and there
was a certain nervous energy around them. They were too
dressed up and everybody was staring at them and they
knew it. They also loved it.

"Wouldn't you love to fuck that? You take the one with
the tits and I'll take the tall one. Then we'll switch. Look
at them. Jesus! They're just made to be fucked."

They were all-right-looking if you liked giraffes.

Frank went on, "I own this place. You know what that
does to girls? C'mon, let's get them over here. Jesus!
Look at their butts!"

"Frank, what happened between you and Gloria?"

"Oh, fuck Gloria. Look at the tits on that one! I have to
have her. Jesus!" He poured more scotch into his glass
and drank some of it. The bottle was almost empty. My
guess was that he'd had the whole thing, and if my guess
was right, he wasn't going to last much longer. He looked
down at his glass as if he had been thinking the same
thing.

"Gloria's a fucking bitch," he said finally. "You know
something? I gave that bitch everything. There wasn't a

thing she wanted that I didn't give her. And sometimes I wonder about myself. How could I have been so fucking blind? She's a fucking ball-buster, that's what she is. A sweet little piece of ass that busts your balls."

I didn't say anything, hoping he would continue, and he did.

"You know something? I should've seen it coming. You know, when I first started fucking her she used to have a cigarette between each fuck. Then one day I realized she was fucking me in between her cigarettes. I should have seen it coming."

"Seen what coming?"

"She overstepped her bounds."

"How'd she do that?"

"You ask too many goddamned questions, you know that? Can't you see I'm drunk as a skunk?" He finished off his glass and drained the rest of the bottle into it. "Let me ask you a question for a change."

"All right."

"You're the one who found Tony. What happened to the five thousand dollars I'd given him? The police said he didn't have a penny on him. Even junkies can't spend money that fast."

I had to smile. It made perfect sense. Whether it was payment for Tony's work with The Merk or it was money to keep him quiet didn't really matter. The big rich drug smuggler gives his junkie brother five thousand dollars, and he dies with it in his shoe. It was just perfect.

I looked at Frank and kept smiling. "I took it," I said.

"Well, where is it?"

"I donated it to a good cause."

"You mean you stole it?"

"It was Tony's to do with what he wanted. I did what Tony would have wanted me to do."

"What'd you do, buy drugs?" And he started laughing.

"Frank, how come you haven't gone after the Chinese? Or did you kill The Merk because you thought he killed Tony?"

He downed his drink and stuck his chin out toward me.

I thought he was going to pass out, but he turned his head and looked off toward the bar. Lenny of the outboard-motor oil appeared at the table again.

"Get him out of here," Frank said.

Lenny grabbed my arm real tight and stood me up.

"Frank, I'm on your side. I can help you."

"Bullshit. Get him out of here." And his head collapsed on the table, knocking the empty bottle onto the floor. It hit with a crash and suddenly everyone was staring at Lenny leading me out toward the fire exit in the back.

"It's all right, Lenny," I said. "I'm going."

"I just want to make sure," he said.

"I think Frank had too much to drink."

"You think so, huh?"

"Does he always drink that much?"

"Do you always stick your face where it don't belong?"

I tried to wiggle free of him, but he held on tightly and pushed me through the door into a parking lot. He still held my arm when we got outside and I had a sudden desire to be home in bed, but it was too late.

He took the wind out of me with his first punch and then held me up and took a few good blows at my face with his free hand. Then he dragged me to the back of the lot and left me behind a dumpster, not without a good kick in the groin.

Chapter 13

When I got back Gloria was sitting in the hallway, leaning against the door of my apartment like the envelope I had received that afternoon. She was wearing tight blue jeans and black boots and a blue silky blouse. Her already puffy eyes were red and swollen from crying, and her face was stained with makeup. She stood up when she saw me coming out of the elevator and hid a soiled tissue behind her back. She tried to laugh. "Oh, Eddie," she said as I walked toward her. "I was beginning to wonder if you'd ever come home. Or maybe if Leon had given me the wrong address. It's scary up here." She made another attempt to laugh. "Leon told me that you don't hang out at The Pit anymore. He said you . . . Eddie! What happened to your face?"

"I hurt myself trying to break-dance."

"Eddie, look at you!" She tried to touch me, but I grabbed her arm.

"Don't touch it. It hurts like hell." I opened the door and we went into my apartment.

"Eddie, what happened to you?"

She followed me to the kitchen area, and I pulled some ice out of the freezer and wrapped it in a towel. "I just got back from a visit with your boyfriend . . ." I put the ice pack just below my left eye where the pain was the worst. ". . . and picked up a little door prize at Sanka's."

"Did Frank do that to you?"

"One of his boys did. Hey, what happened between you two anyway?"

"What did Frank tell you?"

109

"Not much." With the ice pack pushed against my face I went into the bathroom and started a bath. Then I took a couple of Valiums out of the medicine cabinet and swallowed them. It was fun being an American. I leaned against the bathroom door and looked at Gloria. She was sitting on the couch with her legs crossed and she was smoking a cigarette. Her right leg on top moved slowly, bouncing her boot up and down in the air. She wasn't crying anymore and I don't know why, but I was glad she was there.

"Listen, Gloria, it hurts for me to talk. I'm going to take a bath and see if I can put myself back together. But my ears still work. Why don't you talk to me while I'm in the bath?"

She smiled. "OK."

When the tub had filled up the water was too hot, but I left it that way. I dumped the ice pack in the sink and got undressed. It took a long time to submerge myself into the boiling kettle, but when I was finally in I felt a little better. I turned the water off and a sudden silence filled my apartment. Through the crack of the bathroom door I could see Gloria's boot bouncing up and down in the air.

"How's the bath?"

"Like heaven."

"Eddie, what did Frank tell you?"

"You were going to do the talking, remember?"

"I'm not ready."

"Have a drink."

"No thanks."

"OK, don't have a drink."

"Frank always says that."

"I know."

"Was he drinking a lot, Eddie?"

"Yeah." I took a washcloth and gently patted my face. The water made my skin sting. I put the whole cloth over my face and held my breath and counted to fifty. Then I wet the cloth and did it again. It didn't hurt so much the second time.

"Eddie, what did Frank say about me?"

"He said you were a bitch."

"What else?"

"He said a lot. But he was drunk and it didn't make any sense. He said you overstepped your bounds. What the hell happened anyway?"

"Eddie, I'm sorry about what happened at the funeral."

"You mean the slap?"

"I don't know what got into me."

"Oh, come on. You didn't come here to apologize for that."

"I know. I just wanted to tell you that I was sorry. You want me to come in there and wash your face for you?"

"No. Thanks."

"Are you sure?"

I wasn't the least bit sure, but I said, "Yeah, thanks."

"I never loved anyone like I loved Frank."

"Not even Tony?"

"Not even Tony. Tony was fun and wild, but Tony treated me like shit. You know that. Tony liked the idea of me, but he never took the time to find out who I was. He didn't care about me. All he cared about was himself. He didn't miss me when it was over. He never felt anything for me."

"That's not the story I heard."

"Oh, he might have thought he loved me, and he was always jealous if I flirted with someone else, but he didn't really care."

"And Frank did?"

"Frank treated me like gold. I remember the first night he took me out. We went to a Knicks game. He explained the whole game to me and told me who all the players were and how much they got paid. He explained things to me. He taught me things, Eddie. Tony never did that. The only thing Tony ever did was criticize me."

"Did Tony know about you and Frank?"

"Not at first. Nobody did at first."

"Then what happened?"

Her foot disappeared. I heard her walk around and then she sat down again. Her foot was back, but it wasn't bouncing. There was the sound of a match, a moment of silence for an inhale, and then it started bouncing again.

"I don't know. We found out we really loved each other. Frank said he wanted to get married, and that was OK with me, but he had a family. So he was going to get divorced, but it was going to take some time. But we couldn't hide our love anymore."

"The cat was out of the bag."

"I know what you're thinking, Eddie. You think I'm some kind of homewrecker or something. And you think I'm a bitch because it was Tony's brother. But it wasn't like that at all. We just fell in love."

"How did Tony take it?"

"Not so good. He was pretty jealous. They were both always jealous of each other. It's a weird family."

"Did Frank keep you?"

"You mean . . ."

"Did he give you money?"

No answer. Just the black boot bouncing up and down. Then, "Yeah, he gave me money. I mean I wasn't his mistress or anything like that. But he gave me an apartment in one of his buildings on Carmine Street. He gave me enough to live on."

"But you weren't his mistress."

"Is that a statement or a question?"

"So what was the catch? Where'd it go wrong?"

"I want to wait until you get out of the bathtub to tell you."

"Go ahead and tell me now. I can take it lying down."

"It's no joke, Eddie."

I stood up and pulled the drain on the tub. I dried myself and then wrapped the towel around my waist. My whole body was throbbing, but the Valium was starting to set in and I didn't care so much about the pain. I looked at myself in the mirror. I had a rude-looking gash under my left eye, my cheek was swollen and I needed a shave, but otherwise I looked all right. I still had the scar on my forehead from a fight I'd had in high school. My hair was a curly mess on top of my head. Maybe I'd let it grow a

little more this time. My eyes were clear and steady. This
was no drunk I was staring at. This was a man who might
make it, after all.

Wrapped in the towel, I stepped out of the bathroom and
stared at Gloria. She had finished her second cigarette, and
she sat with her arms crossed and her leg still bouncing.
She looked up at me and her leg stopped.

"He killed Tony."

Something was wrong with my mind. All I could do
was think that she was beautiful. I just stood there, half
naked, studying her puffy face and her puckered lips. First
Tony, then Frank. Who would be the next lucky man?

"How do you know?" I heard myself say.

Her leg started bouncing again. "I know."

"Yeah, but how do you know?"

"I just know. That's all."

I went back into the bathroom and pulled on some sweat
pants and a T-shirt. When I came back out she was
smoking another cigarette and her leg was bouncing away
as if she were trying to catapult her boot across the room.

"You don't believe me, do you?" she asked.

"Of course I believe you. I'd believe you if you told me
that Tony was killed by a pack of wild Indians. I'd still
like to know how . . ."

"He told me."

"Frank told you he killed Tony?"

"That's right."

"Is that why you broke off with him?"

"He killed his own brother, Eddie! He's a monster. I
knew he was involved in all kinds of shit and that sometimes he had to take care of people. I knew what kind of
shit he was into. But I didn't care. That was his business
and I loved him. But he killed his own brother, Eddie. I
can't handle that. I can't love a man who would kill his
own brother. It makes me sick."

"So you left him."

"I had to, Eddie, can't you see that?"

"Why did he kill him?"

She took a deep drag of her cigarette. "This is where it gets really sick."

"Did it have to do with The Merk or Gus Harper?"

She shook her head "No. He killed him because he was jealous."

"Jealous of Tony?"

She nodded.

"What were you doing, going out with both of them or something?"

"No! I was going out with Frank. OK, I saw Tony every once in a while. Frank just wouldn't believe me that there was nothing between me and Tony anymore."

"Was there?"

"No! I saw him once in a while, that was it. I swear it!"

I pulled the old cop trick of staring right into her eyes. She couldn't look at me and finally she said, "OK, so I was with him once."

"When?"

"I don't know. A few months ago. It was no big deal. I wasn't going to say anything to Frank. Tony must have opened his big mouth. And Frank killed him. The whole thing makes me sick."

"Why don't you go to the police?"

"Oh, c'mon, Eddie. You know they aren't going to do anything."

"Well, what are you going to do?"

She started to cry. "I don't know. I thought you could tell me what to do. I'm so confused, Eddie."

I stood over her and let her cry. That's what women do when their hearts have been broken. Men drink until they can't see and then they cry. Women cry until they have no tears left. Then they drink. There was no sense pushing her, but I tried anyway. "You want a drink?"

"No."

Something gnawed at the back of my brain. Frank killed Tony. He'd killed Tony and all along he hadn't said anything. Of course, he wasn't going to tell the world about it, but it had to be with him all the time. At Sanka's while he was drinking. At the funeral. Before the funeral. There was something wrong with that. I had thought that Frank killed The Merk to avenge Tony's death. OK, so someone else killed The Merk. Or Frank did it for some other reason. Still, something was scratching away like a rat trying to get out of a shoe box.

"What are we going to do, Eddie?" Gloria was still crying.

"We need to get some help. I've got to talk to the old man."

"Who?" she said through her sobs.

"The old man. Tony's father."

"No, Eddie. I don't want him to know. It would kill him."

"But it's our only hope. We can't do this without some help."

She sat up and held back her crying. "We can't talk to him, Eddie."

"Why not?"

"They won't let you."

"Who won't let me?"

"Frank."

"I'm not gonna ask Frank."

"You have to ask Frank. Frank keeps him locked up in that house. Frank hires all the servants. They all work for Frank."

"Well, then I'll call him."

"They won't let you talk to him."

"OK. Then you'll call him."

"No, Eddie."

"Why not?"

"I'm scared." And she started crying again.

"Shit. You want me to tell you what you should do?" She kept crying.

"We've got to talk to the old man. He's the only one who can help us."

"I can't, Eddie! I'm scared."

"Scared of what?"

"You're playing with fire."

I brought the telephone over to her and put it on her lap. "Call him."

"It's too late, Eddie."

"We'll wake him up. It's important. Call him."

"I don't know the number."

"Bullshit!"

"Eddie, why are you doing this to me?" She was crying and staring down at the phone on her lap. "Why can't you leave me out of it? Just leave me alone."

"Listen, Gloria." I knelt down in front of her and took her hands. "You came here to tell me that Frank killed Tony. You want me to do something. That's why you're here. Now I can't just go to the police 'cause they'll laugh me out of the station. And I can't take Frank on myself because he's got too many men around him all the time. I need help, and only Mr. Santucci is going to help me. I talked to him. He wants me to find Tony's killer. He told me that. Now you've got to call him."

She was crying uncontrollably. "I can't, Eddie. I'm sorry. I just can't."

I picked up the telephone from her lap and threw it across the floor. "Then don't!"

"Eddie, please . . ."

"Don't help me. I'll do it all myself. You're scared? Let me tell you something. I'm scared too. But that's not going to stop me."

But she was crying so loudly that she couldn't hear me. I sat down in the armchair and let her cry. I felt sorry for her. It would have been easy to go put my arms around her and tell her that everything would be all right. It would be easy to be her hero. But I wasn't ready to do that. Anything I felt for her could come later.

Finally she sat up and blew her nose. Her face was red and her blouse was stained with teardrops. "I loved him, Eddie. He was the best thing that ever happened to me." She lit a cigarette.

"You want a drink?" Still pushing.

"No. Leon said that you don't drink anymore."

"I don't. I gave it up."

"Congratulations." She let out a little laugh. "Do you think that maybe we should let this whole thing go?"

"I don't think I can."

"What can we do?"

"You can call the old man."

"What would I say?"

"Just tell him you have a friend who wants to see his stamp collection."

"They might not let us in."

"Maybe not. But we have to try."

She blew her nose again. Then she went to the bathroom and I heard the water running. She came out drying her face with a towel. "I look like shit."

"You look all right. You look better than I do."

She giggled. "That's not saying much."

She sat down on the arm of the chair next to me. "I always liked you, Eddie."

"I always liked you too."

"You did?"

"Sure."

She hugged me and I hugged her back. It felt warm and real, and I didn't let go when she did. She didn't pull away. She just sat there with my arms around her.

"Eddie?"

"What?"

"Do you ever think about leaving New York?"

"All the time."

"Where would you go?"

"I don't know. I guess back to Florida."

"That's where you're from, isn't it?"

"Yeah."

"Did you like it down there?"

"Not when I was there, I didn't. I was bored all the time. I used to drink a lot and sit out on the docks and watch the boats."

"Is that why you came to New York?"

"Yeah. One night I just couldn't make myself go back to the trailer."

"The trailer?"

"Yeah, we lived in a trailer."

"Really?"

"Really. So I spent the night sleeping on the dock outside this bar called Alabama Jack's. I slept out there every night for a week until one night my father came out and sat down next to me. It wasn't like him to do that. It wasn't like him to pay much attention to what I was doing. It's not that he didn't love me. It's just the way he is. So we sat there all night and drank together. We didn't talk much. And in the morning he told me to leave. He told me that I could waste my life if I wanted to, but he didn't want to watch. He gave me five hundred dollars and I came to New York."

"Do you miss him?"

"Sometimes."

We sat there not saying anything for a while. I guess I was thinking about my father. Maybe when this was all over, I'd go down and visit him.

Then Gloria stood up. "I think I'll have that drink now. Do you mind?"

"Not at all. There's probably still some booze in the cabinet over the sink."

"You want something, Eddie?"

"No."

"Oh, I'm sorry. I forgot." She poured herself some brandy that I didn't even know I had and sat back down next to me. "It's too late to call him now, Eddie. We'll call him first thing in the morning."

"OK."

"Eddie?"

"What?"

"Can I sleep on your couch? I don't feel like going home tonight. I don't feel like being alone. Is that all right?"

"Sure. Why don't you sleep on the bed and I'll sleep on—"

"No, no, no. I don't want to put you out. You need a good night's rest. I'll be fine. Just get me a pillow and a blanket."

Later I stretched out in bed and she was on the couch with all the lights out. I couldn't see her, but it felt good to know she was there.

"Eddie?"

"Yeah."

"What happened when you saw Frank tonight?"

"Not much. I asked too many questions and one of his bouncers threw me out into the parking lot."

"What did he tell you?"

"He was pretty drunk. I think he was thinking about you. Or trying not to think about you."

"That hurts."

"Sorry."

"What'll they do to him if they get him?"

"I don't know. Throw him in jail, I guess."

Then I drifted off to sleep and somewhere in dream world a soft warm body floated into my bed and ran her smooth hands all over my body. My body was still sore and sometimes it hurt, but I didn't let on because I didn't want the hands to stop touching me. And then in the total darkness her body gently rolled on top of me and she slipped her warm wet tongue in my mouth and pulled me inside her and our bodies rocked back and forth slowly in a semiconscious dream.

Chapter 14

I was going blind. I was driving a jeep on a grassy road in the jungle with my father. The road was completely overgrown and it was hard to see where it went. I kept following the tracks of other people's mistakes, and I'd have to back up and try again. My father kept trying to tell me which way to go, but it wasn't my father anymore, it was Tony's father. It was hard to see out from under my eyelids. The road finally disappeared altogether. There was just grass everywhere. We got out to figure out what to do. I was trying to look for tracks, but I couldn't see. Now Tony's father was Detective Murphy. He said, "You don't know what you're doing, Margolis." I kept walking but my eyes hurt and I was scared because I was going blind . . .

I had forgotten to close the shades and I woke up with the sun in my eyes. The window was open and a cool late-August breeze swept through the apartment. I lay in bed relieved that I could see and wondering if there had been a road under all that grass. I hadn't even realized that Gloria was missing when the bathroom door popped open and she came out, wrapped in a towel and dripping wet. Her hair was down past her shoulders when it was wet and it was a little bit darker than usual, but still blond. She had no makeup on, and her face was clean and shiny. My eyes traveled down to her neck and shoulders, which glistened with small sparkling drops of water. The towel hugged her body closely, pushing her breasts together and outlining her hips.

And then there were her legs. I had seen longer legs and

I had seen skinnier legs. I had even seen shapelier legs. But I had never seen more sensuous legs. They were strong without being muscular. They looked smooth and warm. They weren't anything less than perfect.

"Well, look who's up," she said. She stood at the foot of my bed smiling.

"Good morning."

"I hope you don't mind that I took a shower. You want some breakfast?"

"Sure."

But she didn't move. She just stood there in the towel and let me look at her. She wasn't being seductive, she was being nice.

"We got to go soon, Eddie."

"Go where?"

"New Jersey. I called Tony's father and he's expecting us."

"What'd you tell him?"

"Just what you told me to."

"And he bought it?"

"It was a cinch. Of course, we still have to get past the servants."

"Well, one step at a time."

"I hope you know what you're doing, Eddie."

She disappeared back into the bathroom, and I got up and got dressed. When she came out she was dressed and smoking a cigarette. "I used the pink toothbrush. I figured that was the right one. You know, Eddie," she continued, going into the kitchen and opening the refrigerator, "when this is all over I think I'd like to get out of New York for a while."

"Where would you go? Here, I'll make some coffee."

"I don't know. I sure as hell don't want to go back to Iowa."

"Iowa? I thought you were from Chicago."

She laughed "So did everyone else. I used to be embarrassed to say I was from Iowa."

"Iowa, huh?"

"Yeah, can you believe it? Is scrambled all right?"

"Fine. How'd you end up in New York?"

"That's a long story."

And over breakfast she told me.

"I had a boyfriend named Robert Smith. Can you believe it? Robert Smith. We called him Buddy. He was a singer and a musician. You know, country music. He used to play all the bars in Iowa. He even played in Chicago a few times. Oh, I guess he was pretty good, but I thought he was the next Hank Williams." She took a forkful of eggs and a couple of bites of toast.

"Anyway, he got it in his head that if he was going to make it he'd have to go to Nashville, and that in order to make it in Nashville, he'd have to make it first in New York. I don't remember how he figured that out, but at the time it seemed to make sense. So I saved my money for two years from working as a cocktail waitress at this steak place. A thousand dollars I saved. That was a lot back then."

"It still is, in the circles I travel in."

"So we came to New York. I guess that was in 1977. Our first night here we went to CBGB's. Oh boy, Eddie, you should've seen us. Him with his cowboy boots and cowboy shirt and me with my farmer's dress and some silly little hat I used to wear all the time. We must have looked ridiculous. The bands were loud and I didn't understand them, and all I wanted to do was go back to our room. But Buddy. Buddy just sat there and watched the bands and drank beer. I don't know who was playing. I think it might have even been The Revelons or someone. I just remember I kept pleading with Buddy to take me out of there, but we stayed until four in the morning. It was one of the worst nights of my life."

She pushed the half-full plate of food away and lit a cigarette. "Then we got back to the room, some sleazy little room in some fleabag hotel. Buddy just sat up all night and played his guitar, trying to figure out all those punk chords and stuff. It was like country music had never existed. He wouldn't come to bed with me and he fell asleep on the floor with all of his clothes on."

She poured us both more coffee and continued. "Well, that was it. Buddy gave up me and country music, and it was all over. He just left me flat for a new life of punk rock and girls with tattoos. I'll never forgive him for that. I saved all my money to bring him to New York and he just dumped me flat."

"What ever happened to him?"

"Oh, he started some band called Don't Stop Now or something like that. They did all right for a while, but I don't know what ever happened to him."

"And you?"

"I was pretty depressed for a while. I hung out at CBGB's a lot, hoping to see Buddy. And I started getting into getting picked up. You know, I was indoctrinated into New York like everyone else."

"And then you met Tony."

"Well, you know the rest after that."

We sipped our coffee and she lit another cigarette. Gloria Joplin, a small-town girl from Iowa, now in the big city going out with drug smugglers like Frank Santucci. Maybe she was the road I had been looking for in my dream. Or maybe she was just somebody else's mistake. It didn't matter. Thinking about how she had climbed into my bed in the middle of the night made my heart race a little bit faster.

Gloria drove us out to Englewood Cliffs in her Mustang, which she admitted had been a gift from Frank. The first time I had seen Tony's father's house had been at the reception after the funeral, and now the empty parking area at the end of the driveway and the enormous wooden front door locked up tight gave me an uneasy feeling. I think Gloria felt it too and she grabbed my arm before I got out of the car.

"Eddie, will you be careful?"

"Of course."

"No, I mean if we can't get in, let's just go away. Don't do anything stupid."

"Just leave it to me."

"No, Eddie. I'm scared."

"What are you scared of?"

"I don't know. I just don't want there to be any trouble."

We got out of the car and climbed the steps to the front door, and Gloria rang the bell. Nothing happened. She rang it again and the door opened immediately, as if they were waiting for the second ring. A man's face appeared in the crack of the door. One of his eyebrows seemed permanently raised and his lips drooped in a frown of disapproval.

"Yes?"

"Hi, Joey!" Gloria said.

He opened the door a little bit more and looked at her. He was tall and not quite as old as he had seemed at first. "Hi, Gloria." It was a friendly start.

"We're here to see Mr. Santucci," she said.

"He's not here, Gloria."

"But I spoke to him this morning. I told him I was coming. He's expecting me."

"I'm sorry, Gloria. He's not here."

"Where'd he go?" I asked.

He looked at me as if I were a first-grader who had just spoken out of turn. "I'm afraid I couldn't say."

"You couldn't say?"

He kept looking at me. "I don't know where he went, Mr. Margolis."

So he knew my name. Big deal. I knew his. "When will he be back?"

"I'm afraid I couldn't . . . I don't know."

"Joey, don't play games with us," Gloria said. "I spoke to him this morning. I know he's here. Did Frank tell you not to let us in?"

"I'm sorry, Gloria. Mr. Santucci is not here."

"OK," I said. "We'll wait for him." I put my hand against the door and tried to push it open. It was like trying to straighten the Leaning Tower of Pisa.

"No can do."

"Oh, come on, Joey!" Gloria said.

"Don't push me, Gloria. He's not here and you can't come in."

"Fine," I said. "We'll wait right here." I turned around and sat down on the top step. I heard the door slam behind me, and Gloria came up and sat next to me. She lit a cigarette and inhaled half of it.

"Now what?" she asked.

"We wait."

"Eddie, I know he's in there. He never goes anywhere."

"Of course he's there."

"Then what are we waiting for?"

"I don't know yet. I'll tell you when it happens."

"Let's get out of here."

"No, we're going to wait."

"We could be here all day."

"Can the old man hear the door from his study?"

"I don't know."

"Think! You've probably been in the house a hundred times. If you're sitting in the study with the door closed, can you hear the front doorbell?"

"Eddie, I don't know! Please, let's get out of here. I'm scared."

"I'm scared too."

"Well, then let's get out of here."

"You know, it's a funny thing I've just realized in the past few days. I'd rather be scared than bored."

She didn't say anything. The birds and the crickets sang songs to each other and the wind rustled the leaves in applause. There were no other sounds except Gloria blowing out cigarette smoke. She was going to be a problem if it turned out to be a long wait.

"Who's Joey?" I asked.

"He works for Frank. He keeps an eye on Mr. Santucci. I guess he's the chauffeur or the butler or something."

"You know him well?"

"No."

"You get along with him?"

"I don't know him well enough to say."

She dropped her cigarette and ground it out with her foot. Then she lit another one.

"Eddie, let's go. I don't—"

"Shhhh!"

"What is it, Eddie?"

"Did you hear that?"

"Hear what?"

"Listen."

It was very soft, but it was clear. A light tapping sound, as if someone were banging a fingernail on a window. Five short taps and then silence. If it happened once I wouldn't have noticed it, but it continued. Five short taps and then silence. I stood up and tried to trace the sound. It came from somewhere toward the side of the house. Five short taps and then silence.

"C'mon," I whispered to Gloria. She got up, and I took her hand and led her toward the side of the house. The taps grew louder. In the last window before the corner of the house I saw the old man. He pointed toward the side of the house and then disappeared.

I led Gloria around the side of the house, her hand squeezing mine. For a minute I thought about how nice it would be to hold her hand and go to a movie. For some reason I pictured us standing in line for popcorn at the old movie theater in Homestead. We were going to see a Clint Eastwood movie.

A door opened from the side of the house and the old man appeared. He was wearing an old pair of tweed pants that were held up by a pair of bright red suspenders. He had on a clean white button-down shirt with the collar open. Large tufts of white hair poured out from his chest. He put a finger to his lips and winked, and he held the door open for us as we stepped into the study I had seen the day of the funeral.

He closed the outside door and turned around to look at us. "Sit down, my friends."

Gloria gave him a kiss on the cheek and sat down in a big chair. The old man led me by the arm over to a couch and then, half leaning on me for support, sat down. I sat next to him.

"You've met Eddie Margolis, Mr. Santucci?" Gloria asked.

"Sure, sure. He was a friend of my Tony's."

"That's right, Mr. Santucci," I said.

"We had a little chat in the garden, didn't we?"

"That's right."

He sat up and looked pleased with himself. "Not bad for a senile old geezer like myself, huh?"

"You have an excellent memory, Mr. Santucci," Gloria said.

He smiled sadly. "Oh, you don't have to kid me, Gloria. I'm losing my mind and everyone knows it. They all talk to me like I'm some kind of a deaf idiot. Maybe I am. But sometimes this old noodle still pulls through. What happened to your face, Mr. Eddie?"

"I got in an accident."

"With a couple of fists it looks like. Would you like something to drink? A lemonade perhaps?"

"I'd love a lemonade," Gloria said.

"Good." He pushed a button on the table next to him and the door opened. Joey's eyes sank into the back of his head when he saw us.

"Hi, Joey!" I said. I couldn't resist.

"Get us three lemonades, would you, Joey?" the old man asked.

Joey walked out without saying a word. I winked at Gloria and she smiled.

"No, the young ones don't come around much anymore," the old man said. "Used to be a time when you kids would visit every Sunday. I know. There's not much to say to an old man like me. Sometimes I wake up in the morning and I try to figure out what day it is. And then I try to remember what I did the day before. And I can't remember a single thing about the day that's just passed. It's a scary feeling, like you're floating in time. Have you met my son Frank?"

My hand went instinctively to my face.

"Oh, yes. I see you have. He still visits. Brings the family, his beautiful wife and those two little brats whose names I never remember." Joey came in with the lemonades on a tray and the old man kept talking. "Frank's a good son. He's never let me down, like the other one. He keeps a good eye on me too. Maybe he's a little bit overly protective.''

Joey placed the tray down on the table in front of us.

''Wouldn't you say he was overly protective, Joey?''

''I wouldn't know, sir.''

''Oh, yes you would. Wouldn't you say that turning my friends here away at the door was overly protective?''

''I didn't turn them away, sir. I merely . . .''

''Oh, get out of here and go take up your post.''

''My post, sir?''

''Yes, your post. Leaning your ear against the door like Frank tells you to.''

''Oh, I wouldn't—''

''Sometimes I feel like a prisoner in my own house. Go on, get out of here.''

Just before Joey slipped out the door he turned around and looked at me. Gloria and the old man were busy reaching for their lemonades. Joey smiled at me in a haunting way and drew a finger across his throat. I felt a chill run down my spine. Joey was going to be a problem.

''Gloria, has your friend seen the garden?''

''Yes, you showed me the garden, Mr. Santucci.''

''Oh.''

We drank our lemonades and the old man seemed to drift off somewhere.

''Mr. Santucci,'' I said. ''I was hoping you'd be able to tell me something about why your son was killed.''

He drifted back. ''Frank?''

''No, Tony.''

Gloria coughed to get my attention and then shook her head and nodded toward the door. Joey would be listening.

''He used to visit me every Sunday with his girl friend Gloria,'' the old man was saying.

''I'm right here, Mr. Santucci,'' Gloria said.

He looked at Gloria and sort of squinted. It was sad to watch his mind playing tricks with him.

''I was hoping to show you my stamp collection, Mr. Eddie.''

I took the lemonade out of his hand and pulled him up off the couch. His hands were smooth and shiny, and they still had strength in them. I followed him as he walked slowly to the big mahogany desk.

"Do you like stamps, Mr. Eddie?"

"I don't know."

"What do you like?"

"Fishing."

He stopped and shook my hand. "I love a fisherman. We'll have to talk fishing later. Anyone who likes to fish should like stamps. You've got to have something to do when you're not fishing."

He pulled a large green stamp album off a book shelf and laid it down on the desk. "Here, I want to show you something." He flipped through the pages. The album was filled with colorful old stamps, all mounted precisely in slick little black mounts. Each page looked perfect. He turned toward the front of the album, where the stamps were older. They were still in mint condition, uncanceled and clean, and the perforations were perfectly cut. They were as perfect as Gloria's legs.

"There's one in particular I want to show you, Mr. Eddie. Let's see if I can find it."

"They're all beautiful, Mr. Santucci."

"Yes, but I want you to see my favorite."

I stood there while he flipped the pages back and forth. It seemed as if we kept looking at the same pages. They all had names and dates at the top. We were looking at pages with stamps from 1935 to 1940.

"What year is it?" I asked, trying to be helpful.

"Well . . ." He turned a few more pages. "I'm not really sure now. That's what I can't remember." More page turning. I suppressed a yawn and waited. "I thought it was right here. I was just looking at it this morning."

I don't know how long I stood there while he flipped pages back and forth, but it seemed like an hour. I looked back at Gloria. Her eyes were teary. She put a finger to her lips and shook her head.

"Ah!" he said at last, and he laid the album open to a page labeled "National Parks, 1934."

"These are not the most expensive stamps in the world, by any means, Mr. . . ."

"Eddie."

"But they happen to be my favorites."

Each stamp, maybe ten of them on the page, had a beautiful landscape and the name of a national park. "They're beautiful," I said.

"Here's my favorite," he said, pointing to one of Crater Lake. "Look closely at the detail." And then with a pair of tweezers he very carefully lifted the bottom part of the mount off the page. The top part stuck to the page, but underneath the bottom part something was scribbled in pencil. It was very difficult to make out.

"Here, look with this." He handed me a magnifying glass. "Study it closely, Mr. Eddie. You see the lines and the color?" I leaned forward and looked through the magnifying glass, and suddenly I could read the scribble as clear as day: "Chinatown—August 5; Auction—September 5." I looked at it for a long time. Then the old man took the magnifying glass from my hand and put an eraser to the page. The words were gone.

I knew he was trying to tell me something, but I didn't know what it was. We sat back down on the couch.

"What does it all mean?" I asked.

"Stamps are beautiful, aren't they?" he asked. "They're history and art and purpose all together, printed on a tiny piece of paper."

"Yeah, but . . ."

"Oh, you young men are headstrong and rambunctious. You can't appreciate the detail and the history. Sometimes you don't understand that things have got to be handled very delicately. You say you're a fisherman, Mr. Eddie?"

I wasn't sure if we were talking about Tony or not, but I played along. "I love to fish."

"What, in your opinion, is the single most important aspect of catching fish?"

"The fight."

"No, no, no. I mean how to catch them."

"Oh. Being in the right spot?"

"No, I don't think so."

"Time of day?"

"No."

"Bait."

"Exactly! Go to any spot you want any time of the day and you can catch fish if you have the right bait."

"I've heard it said that if you're in the right spot at the right time it doesn't matter what kind of bait you have."

He laughed. "That's very good. But I'm the old man so you listen to me. You can't always choose where and when to fish. Not even you young men. Did you ever fish for great northern pike?"

"Sure. My father used to bring me up to Canada every year for a week."

"Good, good. Let's say you're jigging for pike with some live bait. Something good. Your line is loose, just floating along the bottom. Then suddenly the line gets tight and it starts going out. What do you do?"

He wasn't asking me. He was testing me. "You let him take it."

"Good!" He glanced at Gloria approvingly and said with a smile, "This guy really knows his fishing." Then to me, "OK, so he's taking it. What happens if you pull the line?"

"You pull it out of his mouth."

"Exactly!"

"So how do you get him?" Gloria asked.

"Tell her, Mr. Eddie."

"You wait until he stops moving."

"What does that mean, when he stops moving?" The old man was getting excited, as if we were out on the boat.

"It means he's swallowing it."

"What do you do?"

"Nothing. You let him swallow it."

"And how do you know when he's swallowed it?"

"He starts moving again."

"And then?"

"You set the hook!" I pulled my hands up with an imaginary fishing rod. I guess I was right out there on the boat with him.

"Good! Excellent! You just caught a real fine fish."

"That sounds like fun," Gloria said.

The old man leaned back on the couch as if he were worn out from a day of fishing. "So, Mr. Eddie, now you've got the bait. You can go fishing. Well, my friends, Gloria, my sweetheart, I'm afraid it's time for my nap."

"It was good to see you again, Mr. Santucci," Gloria said.

"Next time I'll show you my garden. I'd better see you to the door."

The old man led us through the study, down the long hallway with the chairs and couches to the front door. Joey met us in the foyer.

"What'd you do, Joey? Take the long way around?" the old man asked.

"It's time for your nap, sir."

"I know it is, Joey. I was just seeing Tony and Gloria to the door."

Joey, Gloria and I exchanged glances. For an instant we shared the embarrassment of the old man's mistake, and we were all on the same side with age and senility as the enemy. We each waited for someone else to correct him, but the old man turned and walked back toward his study before anyone said anything.

"So long, Joey," I said.

Over my shoulder as I walked out the door I heard him say, "So long is right, Margolis."

Chapter 15

It was a fun ride back to the city. We talked about the old times and the clubs, and we laughed a lot. It was another crystal-clear summer day and we crossed the George Washington Bridge with the windows open and the air rushing through the car. Manhattan was stretched out below us sparkling in the sunlight. Driving down the West Side Highway, or what was left of it, I stared out over the Hudson River and the New Jersey Palisades, and I was overcome with a feeling of reckless jubilation. At a stoplight in front of the aircraft carrier *Intrepid,* I bought two hot pretzels from a street vendor, and we ate them and laughed at ourselves. I don't know if I was falling in love, but I was falling into something.

Gloria drove me to the main branch of the New York Public Library and she pulled up between two busses in front of the large stone stairway on Fifth Avenue. Her hair was pulled back behind her ears and she sat staring over the dashboard at the Fifth Avenue lunchtime traffic.

"Eddie, do you think Mr. Santucci knows about Frank?"

"No."

"What did he say to you when you were looking at the stamps?"

"He gave me a couple of dates. I have to go in there to find out what they mean," I said, pointing up the steps.

"What dates?"

"August fifth and September fifth."

"Oh."

I waited for her to say something, but she didn't.

"Does that mean anything to you?" I asked.

"Sure. August fifth is the night they raided Chinatown."

"You know about that, then?"

"Christ, Eddie! It was in all the papers. What do you think? You think I've been lying to you?"

"No. Just trying to figure things out. What about September fifth?"

"No. I don't know what that is."

The bus in front of us took off down Fifth Avenue and the driver of the one behind us started honking his horn. Gloria didn't move.

"Eddie, can I see you later?"

"Sure. I'll stop by tonight when I'm finished."

"You promise?"

"Promise."

The honking became insistent; I opened the door and got one foot out, but Gloria stopped me. "Eddie, do you think we could get out of New York for a while when this is all over? I don't know. Go to Florida or something?"

No question ever sounded so good. For a moment the honking behind me seemed to stop and all of Fifth Avenue was waiting for my answer. "Sounds great," I said, and I got out and slammed the door. She pulled off and the bus followed her. The driver looked at me when he passed me and gave me the finger. What a friendly town.

I found my way to the periodical room and then to a window with a shingle that said REFERENCE LIBRARIAN. A little old man who could just see over the counter stood talking to a young girl behind the window. From the tone of the girl's voice I could tell that she was getting annoyed. He was probably one of those people who insisted that the library bend its rules and allow him to take out a book with his social security card.

I waited. The man asked another question. I couldn't hear his question, but I heard her response.

"Sir! I've told you five times already!" And then with forced patience and restraint, "You fill out one of those yellow forms on the desk there. You write down all the information. You bring it to the windows around the corner to your left. I don't have any periodicals here. It doesn't matter what you want. I don't have it.''

Then I heard him. "But I told you. I don't have all the information.'' He had a heavy accent, German or Dutch or something.

The girl saw me standing off to the side and she rolled her eyes. "Look, sir. I'm sorry, we're not mind readers. How can we get you what you want if you don't even know what it is?''

"I do know what it is!''

"Then fill out one of the yellow . . .''

"Ah, you keep telling me the same thing!''

"And you keep asking the same question!''

"All right!'' He waved her off and faced me. "I've had enough already,'' he said to me. "I'll go find it myself.'' And he walked away.

I moved up and leaned my arms on the counter. The girl sat there rubbing her temples with her eyes closed. She was young, probably just out of high school, and she wasn't particularly pretty, but she was pleasant-looking. Her mouth had sort of a sexy twist to it. Then she opened her eyes. They were big and dark, and suddenly she was very pretty, but she was the kind of a girl that boys would take for granted until one of them was smart enough to see what he had.

She smiled at me. "I'm sorry,'' she said. "That man gave me such a headache.''

"Yeah, he gave me a headache, too.''

She kept smiling. "What can I do for you?''

"I need to know where I can find newspapers from August fifth and sixth.''

"Just this past August fifth and sixth?''

"Yeah.''

"Let's see. Those won't be on microfilm yet. Just fill out one of those yellow slips on the desk and . . .''

"I know, I know. Write down all the information and bring it to the windows around the corner to my left. You don't have to tell me again. You told the other guy five times.''

She giggled. "Could you believe him?"

"I'll believe anything. I also need to know where your subject indexes are."

"Around the corner to your right."

"Can you look up someone's name in that index?"

"Sure, you can look up anything."

"Yeah, but will I find anything?"

"Well, that all depends on whose name you look up."

"How's your headache?"

"It's better. Thank you."

"Thank you."

The first part was easy. In fifteen minutes I had the August fifth and sixth editions of all the daily newspapers in New York. And it didn't take long to find the articles in each one about the raid in Chinatown on the night of the fifth. It had occurred at a small bar called The Night Dragon, which was the hangout for members of one of Chinatown's youth gangs, the Black Tigers. Someone had gone in with a machine gun and shot the place up, killing five and wounding eight. *The New York Times* said that at present there were no suspects, but that gang war was suspected. *The Daily News* said that no information was available on the Black Tigers because they were so new, but that Chinese youth gangs usually worked under the umbrella of the Chinese Triads, and that they were notorious for extortion, gambling, prostitution and drugs. *The Post* had big photos of bodies being carried away from The Night Dragon.

The second part was harder. First I looked up Gus Harper's name in the subject index. I went from the present back to 1970. There were only two Gus Harpers. One was an ice-hockey player and the other was some doctor from Texas who had performed open-heart surgery.

Then I looked up the First Star Savings Bank. There were about five pages of listings for references to the First Star Savings Bank for each year. I decided to check only *The New York Times* and only in the last five years. That narrowed it down to about twenty articles. I filled out a yellow slip for each article and then made myself comfortable for some real homework. I hadn't sat in a library for over five years and felt as if I were back in school.

I learned a lot about First Star Savings Bank. In the early sixties First Star Savings Bank grew, almost overnight, into one of New York's largest savings institutions. At the heart of its growth was its owner and president Charles P. Wolfe. First Star was sold to some national bank in the early seventies for a record seven and a half billion dollars. Then in the late seventies it became apparent to the purchaser that there were certain "latent inconsistencies" in the record-keeping practices of First Star and a private investigation was undertaken. The new owner reported "glaring misrepresentations" in First Star's assets and this led to a civil suit against Wolfe, as well as to independent investigations by the attorney general's office and the New York banking board. The preliminary report from the attorney general's office was due out in three days when Charles P. Wolfe drove his custom-made Jaguar over a cliff in California. His wife, Nadine Cynthia Wolfe, miraculously survived the crash and several articles mentioned the curious disappearance of Wolfe's body. Nadine was even held for questioning upon her release from the hospital, but the mystery was ended when Wolfe's body washed up on shore two weeks later.

I turned the microfilm projector off and looked at the big clock on the far wall. I had been there for over three hours. I was an expert on the last days of Charles Wolfe's life, as well as an expert on the "latent misrepresentations" of First Star Savings Bank. I hadn't taken any notes, but I didn't need to. I remembered everything I had read. And yet there was something missing.

I was leaning back in my chair and staring at the ceiling when I heard a voice behind me.

"Did you find what you wanted?"

It was the girl from the reference window.

"Sort of."

"Sort of?"

"Here, look at this." I flipped the machine back on to an article about the appearance of Wolfe's body. It pretty much told the whole story. "Read this and tell me what you think." I moved out of the way and she read over my shoulder.

"Sounds like a real crook," she said when she finished.

"What else?"

"I don't know. What do you want to know?"

"There's something wrong."

"Well, anyone can see that."

"What is it? What's wrong?"

"He died just before the world found out what a crook he was."

"So what?"

"So he knew what was going to be in the attorney general's report and fixed his own death. Frankly, I wouldn't be surprised if that body they found wasn't his at all. I wouldn't be surprised if he were still alive in Argentina or someplace. Just got up and left. Just like that."

I shut off the machine and stared at her. "What did you say?"

"I said he was probably in Argentina or someplace like that."

"Yeah, that he got up and left. Then what did you say?"

"Yeah, that he got up and left. Just like that."

"Just like that."

"Well, I hope you—"

"Wait, wait, wait." I flipped the projector back on and turned back to an article on the crash and his obituary. "What's wrong with this obituary?"

"I told you already. He probably—"

"No, no. Something else. What's wrong with the obituary itself? With the newspaper. Jesus! I've been reading articles about the guy for three hours and I haven't seen his picture yet."

"Maybe he was camera-shy."

"Where can I find a picture of him?"

"Well, it says here that he graduated from Columbia in 1954. They might have his picture in the yearbook."

"Where?"

"I don't know. I think they may have them upstairs somewhere."

I shut the machine off. "C'mon, show me."

"I'm not sure where they are," she said, following me. "I gotta go now. You can . . ."

"Just tell me who to ask."

"Ask the answer man, Mr. Poltrack. We call him the answer man because he knows everything."

"Show me where to find him."

She brought me to a little office up on the third floor. Mr. Poltrack was putting his jacket on and turning off the light on his desk at the same time. He was running to catch a train, but he told me that they did have Columbia yearbooks and he told us where they would be. The girl didn't even have to be asked. She led me up a flight of steps into a dark and dusty room with rows of books and no tables. She led me right to the stack with the Columbia yearbooks.

I pulled down Columbia 1954. The students' photographs were arranged alphabetically and I turned to the W's in the back. The girl looked on as I flipped the pages looking for Charles P. Wolfe and she found him first. "There he is!" she said. And there, clear as day, looking a little younger and healthier, with the crew cut of those days, was Gus Harper.

"He doesn't look like a crook," she said.

And suddenly I realized what I had done. I didn't mind knowing what I was not supposed to know. But now she knew too, even if she didn't know that she knew. If I tried to scare her or swear her to secrecy, she would be that much more inclined to spill the beans to the wrong person.

I closed the book and put it back on the shelf. "Oh well," I said. "I guess I can't use a picture in my report."

"Report?" Her voice showed the disappointment that I was hoping for. "What's your report on?"

"International banking laws and federally insured savings institutions in periods of high inflation."

"Oh." And she scrunched up her face to show her distaste for anything so boring.

"Well, listen. Thanks for your help."

"Sure, anytime."

We walked downstairs together and I asked her about herself just for the hell of it. I was right about her being just out of high school. She was working in the library for the summer and was going to start at City College in a few weeks. I was wrong about the boys, though. She was engaged to be married the following spring. We said good-bye at the bottom of the steps and then I stepped out into rush hour on Forty-second Street.

There are three ways to get a cab in midtown during rush hour. One is to be a jerk and step in front of everybody else as if you didn't see them and take the first cab that comes. Another way is to figure out who's been there before you and wait your turn, and hope that some jerk choosing the first approach doesn't come by before your turn. The third way is to be lucky. That's how I did it. Nobody was around and a cab rolled up to the curb right in front of me and two businessmen got out. I jumped in and we went downtown.

Chapter 16

The narcotics division was on the third floor of the ninth precinct. I pushed the door open and entered a typical city office with maps on the walls, old metal filing cabinets and mounds of paper. A large wooden table stretched the length of the room and was littered with old coffee cups and overflowing ashtrays. A few doors led off to smaller individual offices on the right with windows looking out on the big main room. These outer offices were all dark.

Murphy sat on the far side of the table with his feet up on it and a mug of coffee in his hands. The only other person in the room was Deputy Commissioner Sidney Philips, still dressed for the campaign trail. He was standing on the opposite side of the table from Murphy with his back to the door, and he stopped in mid-sentence and turned around to face me when I came in. He raised his big bushy eyebrows at me and then took a few graceful steps to the side so that Murphy could see me. His eyes darted back and forth between us.

"Well, well, well," Murphy said, without moving. "Look what the wind blew in. What's the matter? Don't you believe in knocking?"

"I've got to talk to you."

Murphy put the mug down on the table and rubbed his face in his hands. "You're doing this on purpose, Margolis."

"Doing what?"

"Coming in here on the worst night of the year and telling me that you have to talk to me. Can't you see I'm in the middle of a meeting? What do I look like? Do I look like I have time to talk to all the riffraff coming in off the street?''

I turned to walk out.

''All right, all right. Get in here,'' he said over my shoulder.

I slammed the door behind me and heard him scream, ''Margolis! Get your ass back in here!''

I kept walking. I heard the door open and his steps behind me. He caught me at the head of the stairs and got past me to block my way. He was out of breath and he looked tired. ''OK, Margolis. You've made your point. I'm tired. I don't know what I'm saying. C'mon in and talk to me.''

I stared at him. He was a big old tired cop with a big square face and a receding hairline. He'd probably seen a lot of things in his time and he probably didn't like to play games anymore, although he still did when he had to. I'd grown up with cops and I knew that there were good cops and bad cops, just like there were good days and bad days. For some reason I liked to think that he was the kind of a cop who would take bribe money and shove it down the briber's throat. I was going to trust him and there was nothing I could do about it.

I followed him back to the office and he pointed to one of the rooms off to the right. His name was on the door. ''Wait in there, Margolis. I'll be with you in a few minutes.''

I sat down at Murphy's desk, since there was no other place to sit, and I didn't put the light on or close the door. His desk was surprisingly neat. There was a perfectly organized tray with paper clips and pens in it. Papers sat squarely in small wooden boxes or in neat little piles on the corners of the desk. There was a framed photograph of his kid, dressed up like a cop. He had a real gun in his hand and a real badge that said ''Sergeant Murphy, Narcotics.''

Out in the main room they started to talk again.

''Look, Sid,'' Murphy said, sitting down in the same chair he had been in before. ''All I'm asking is for twenty-four hours and a handful of new undercovers. Somebody

these people have never seen before. We can get somewhere with this. This is big stuff. Let's not waste it on
filling the joints with junkies.''

"Charlie, I don't know what's the matter with you.
You're supposed to want to clean up the streets, right?
OK! Here's our chance. We're hauling them in faster than
we can book them."

"I don't want the goddamned junkies!" Murphy pounded
his fist on the table.

"What do you want?"

"I told you. I want the big guys."

"Oh, c'mon, Charlie. How are you going to . . .''

"With a couple of undercovers, that's how!"

"I'm sorry. I already told you. We're cleaning up the
streets. Charlie, we got a goddamned riot down there!"

"You know what I think?"

Philips started to pace up and down the length of the
table. "I think you're tired, Charlie."

"I think you're holding back on me. I think you and
everybody else, right on up to the goddamned mayor, are
holding back on me."

"Charlie, you're being ridiculous."

"Maybe, but you haven't said that I'm wrong."

"OK. You want me to tell you that you're wrong?
You're wrong."

"Prove me wrong."

Philips was standing right outside the door of Murphy's
office, and he looked in at me and then casually pulled the
door shut.

Their discussion continued and I could hear the drone of
their voices, but I couldn't make out what they were
saying. Through the window of the office I could see
Murphy with his feet up on the table. Philips kept pacing
back and forth. After a little while Murphy got up and
started to pace on the other side and this made Philips
stand still by the door.

Suddenly Murphy stopped and pounded his fist on the
table. He started screaming and I could hear almost every
word of it. "Damn it, Sid! Look at the desk downstairs!

Count the junkies we locked up today! Look at the goddamned numbers, Sid! They're coming in by the busful
. . . something, something, something. . . . It's a goddamned war zone down there!"

Philips said something and then Murphy continued. "Cit-
ies don't fucking dry up by themselves. Even if you bust
the kingpin, somebody'll move in the next day. You know
that, Sid!"

Again he stopped for Philips's response. Then he started
screaming even more loudly. "You mean to tell me that
you think that this is some kind of fucking natural phe-
nomenon? Some sort of fucking freak accident?"

Philips was squirming by the door.

"Bullshit! You know that's fucking bullshit!" And then
Murphy sat down and spun around in the chair with his
back to Philips. Philips talked for a few minutes, but
Murphy didn't say anything and finally Philips left.

Murphy didn't turn around when the door slammed
behind him. He just sat there with his arms behind his
head, gazing at the wall. He sat like that for a long time.
Finally I got up and walked out of his office. He swiveled
around in his chair when he heard me.

"Remember me?" I asked.

"Yeah, I remember you. Tell me something. What's
it like to be unemployed?"

"It's boring."

"How boring?"

"Really boring."

"How do you eat?"

"I borrow. I get by."

"You must be in quite a fix."

"So what?"

"So, you're young. You can afford to be in a fix. How
old are you?"

"Twenty-six."

"Look at me. I'm almost fifty. I got alimony and child
support up the kazoo. I got mortgage payments, car payments, insurance payments. I'll bet I dish out more in a
month than you see in a year."

"So what?"

"So what am I going to do when I quit this lousy job?"

"Be broke and bored?"

He stuck his feet back up on the table. "Sit down. Let me tell you something. I've had it up to here. Here I am, chief detective of the narcotics division for the ninth precinct. This is a big precinct for narcotics. OK, it ain't Harlem, but it's big. I mean, I should be in there, going after the big guys. We ought to be doing something, for Christ's sake. And Philips, that asshole Philips, the chicken-hearted Mr. Young and Ambitious, ready to set the whole goddamned world on fire, is so fucking stuck with his goddamned procedures and policies that we can't get a fucking thing done. It's all bullshit, Margolis. I've had it up to here."

"What's going on?"

He brought his feet down with a thud and leaned his elbows on the table. "Margolis, I don't know where you've been, but Alphabetland is a goddamned war zone. All of a sudden today the place is crawling with junkies killing each other for nickel bags. Someone cut off the flow of drugs like this." And he snapped his fingers. "Something big is going on down there, Margolis. I can't put my finger on it, but I can smell it. Shit. I'm telling you, I'd go in there myself if I didn't smell like a goddamned cop. And Philips, that asshole, is only interested in cleaning up the junkies. He wouldn't know a once-in-a-lifetime opportunity if it came up and bit him in the ass, which is exactly what it's doing."

We sat there staring at each other. I felt as if there was a tidal wave growing and that I was sitting right on the top of it.

"I can help you get Santucci," I said. He kept looking at me but didn't say anything. "Santucci smuggles smack into the country."

"No shit."

"Santucci delivered to The Merk, who worked for Gus Harper. But Gus Harper doesn't really exist. Gus Harper is really Charles P. Wolfe, an ex-banker . . ."

"Wait a minute, wait a minute, wait a minute. Just hold it, Margolis. Where did you hear all this?"

"I figured it out."

"How?"

"By snooping around."

"Can you prove any of this?"

"Sure, I can."

"How?"

"Well, it all fits together. Wolfe is really . . ."

"Margolis! You're not listening to me. I don't care how it all fits together. I want to know if you have any proof?"

"I can show you where Gus Harper lives. I can show you that he's not Gus Harper, but that his real name is Charles P. Wolfe. I can show you that his wife lives up in a penthouse on Fifth Avenue."

"Can you show me that they're involved in the drugs?"

"How can I show you that?"

"Catch them in the act."

"But they don't act. They have other people do all the work."

He laughed. "Welcome aboard, Margolis. Now you see the fix we're in. Every fucking day."

"So I have to catch them in the act?"

"Yeah. Or you got to get someone to testify. Someone who won't get shot in the process."

"What about a confession?"

That triggered another good laugh. "You kill me, Margolis."

"Can I just tell you what I've found out?"

"Sure, sure. I got all night."

"Tony Santucci and The Merk were acting as spies for Frank Santucci to find out who his competitors were. There was a gang in Chinatown called the Black Tigers. They . . ."

"Were raided a few weeks ago."

"By Frank Santucci."

"How do you know?"

"It's all an effort by Frank Santucci to take control of Gus Harper's operations."

"Santucci led the raid on The Night Dragon?"

"Yup."

"Can you prove it?"

"I'll prove it."

"How?"

He was leaning all the way forward now, drilling away at me with his eyes. He was pushing me like a cop. He needed a good answer. He needed me to do what they wouldn't let him do. He'd throw me to the dogs for Frank Santucci.

"I'll get a confession."

"From who?"

"Frank Santucci."

His face broke into that smirk he had been wearing the first time I saw him. "Margolis, do you know what you're talking about? If you get a confession out of Santucci, you not only make us look like idiots, you make the god-damned FBI look like idiots. I'd love to see it. What have you got? You got something on him?"

"Yeah, I got enough. But I'm going to need help."

"You're damned right you're going to need help."

"I'll want you to be there when he confesses."

"Sure, sure. Why don't you bring him in here and we can all sit around and have tea and take notes?"

"I'm serious. I'm going to nail him."

His smirk disappeared. "Did he kill your friend? Jesus, his own brother? Is that why you want to nail him?"

"That, and this." I pointed to my cheek.

"Yeah, I was wondering about that. And what's this about Gus Harper?"

"His real name is Charles Wolfe."

"In your own words, Margolis, so what?"

"Charles Wolfe was the president of First Star Savings Bank. He was supposed to have died about three years ago. Well, it was all fixed. He's Gus Harper."

"How do you know?"

"I met him."

"You met Gus Harper?"

"That's right."

"Holy fucking shit, Margolis. I got to hand it to you. You've fucking done it. You've actually gone out and impressed me. Now what do you want me to do?"

"I don't know. I thought you'd want to know about all this. I thought it was important."

"Margolis, I'm tired. I've been up since three o'clock this morning. I hate my job. I hate this fucking city. And I hate everything else in this fucking world. Nothing's important to me right now. Except maybe a good night's sleep."

"All right." I stood up. "I'll talk to you later. First, I'll nail Frank Santucci."

"Now wait a minute, Margolis. If you're really serious about getting Santucci, you better know what you're doing. He's not going to hang himself, you know."

"Yes, he is. I'm going to trick him into it."

"And a confession isn't worth a dime unless it's voluntary."

"OK." I started to leave.

"And you've got to have plenty of witnesses. Good witnesses."

"OK."

"Hey, Margolis." I stopped and turned around at the door. "You're a punk, Margolis, but I'm gonna feel sick if you get yourself killed."

I didn't say anything.

"Santucci won't stop for you, you know."

"I know how to handle him."

He smiled slowly. "I hope so. For your sake, Margolis."

Chapter 17

It was getting dark by the time I got to Chinatown. The early-evening sidewalks were crowded with shoppers buying Chinese vegetables and squid from the Canal Street markets, and with tourists wandering among the restaurants and the bakeries. The traffic on Canal Street was backed up from the Manhattan Bridge to the Holland Tunnel, and at times the sidewalks were so congested that I had to walk in the street around the taxis and the trucks. The restaurants on Mott Street advertised their Peking ducks by hanging them upside down in the windows, and dinner lines were already forming outside the more popular restaurants.

When I got down to East Broadway the streets were dark and quiet and there were no tourists. Old tenements lined the streets, their lights shining dimly in the twilight and their doors locked up tight. There were grocery stores and small restaurants, but the streets were empty except for a few Chinese kids smoking cigarettes and hanging out on the corners. There were cats everywhere. Nobody was friendly. At least nobody was friendly to me.

The Night Dragon was a tiny basement bar on a little street just off East Broadway. There was just enough room for a bar and four or five tables. There were a few Chinese at the far end of the bar, talking casually with the bartender. They stopped talking as soon as they saw me and their eyes followed me as I grabbed a stool by the door. The bartender didn't move but eyed me like the others. I felt as out of place as a fork would at the restaurant next door.

The bartender finally sauntered over to where I was

sitting. He was a good-looking Chinese, probably about thirty years old, and his shiny black hair was combed straight back over the top of his head. He spoke with a heavy Chinese accent. "Sorry, we close."

"Good. I was hoping you'd be closed."

He started to say something and then stopped. His eyebrows pushed together and large creases appeared on his forehead. "What is it you want then?"

"The Black Tigers."

His face relaxed and he smiled with the left side of his mouth. "Sorry, I no understand."

"Yes, you do. I'm looking for the Black Tigers."

"I not know how to make that drink. Anyway, we close." He started to walk away.

"It's not a drink. It's a gang," I said to his back. And then, loudly enough for his friends at the other end of the bar to hear, I said, "The Black Tigers. And if you've never heard of them, then you're even dumber than you look because the whole city knows who they are. Even the cops."

His back straightened, and he came back and stood in front of me. "We have no trouble here."

"Good, I don't want trouble. I want the Black Tigers."

"Sorry."

"Not as sorry as you will be."

His forehead creased again. "You threaten me, maybe?"

"Maybe."

"You a cop?"

"No."

"What you want with Black Tigers?"

"I have some information they may be interested in. I'll tell you what I'm going to do. Is that a restaurant next door?"

"Yes."

"OK. I'm going to get some dinner. I'll be there for a while. I'll wait."

"You wait a long time, maybe."

"I got nothing to do." I got off the stool and headed for the door.

I heard him say, "Maybe we find something for you to do."

I turned around to face him. "You threaten me, maybe?"

"Maybe."

Next door was a small Chinese restaurant. I found a little table near the window in the front. I was the only white person there and I was glad to see that the menu was in English as well as Chinese. It was a lively little restaurant filled with the constant chatter of Chinese, the banging of pots and pans and the crackling sizzle of the big woks in the kitchen. It was also hot and steamy, and I drank three glasses of water before I even ordered.

I had an outrageously delicious order of cold noodles and sesame sauce, and I was halfway through a very spicy shrimp with garlic sauce when suddenly I had company.

He couldn't have been older than sixteen. He wore a tie-dyed T-shirt with the sleeves ripped off and there was a thin gold chain around his neck. He had that look that teenagers put on when they want to look tough and when he spoke he sounded as if he were reading a script from an old western. He said, "You want to see the Black Tigers."

"That's right." I took another mouthful of shrimp and chewed slowly. I didn't want to appear overly anxious, and I wanted to finish my shrimp. Clint Eastwood would have finished his shrimp.

"Let's go then."

"I haven't finished my dinner. Or paid the bill."

If he had been more secure, he might have smiled or made a joke. He said, "We'll take care of that. Let's go."

"OK, where to?"

"You follow me."

With a reluctant last glance at my shrimp, I followed him toward the back of the restaurant, through the kitchen and out a door into a stairwell. When the kitchen door swung shut behind us he stuck the point of a gun in my stomach. "Nothing cute now, tough guy," he said. Then he pushed me and we walked up the dark and smelly stairs. "Left," he said when we got to the top. We walked down a hallway with doors on both sides and a kid's tricycle in the middle.

At the end of the hallway there was another set of stairs that we climbed and then ended up on a kind of catwalk that went around the outside of the building. We walked on that until we got to a fire escape; we climbed down the fire escape onto the roof of an adjacent building. We crossed the roof and he pushed me through a door into another building.

We entered a bright room with no windows and only the one door I had come through. It looked like an old storage room, and piles of bricks and pipes lay stacked in the corners behind old folding chairs and an old worn-out couch.

The one with the gun pushed me into the middle of the room and then leaned against the door with the gun in his belt. Nobody said anything, and I walked around in a small circle and looked at them. There were about ten of them. There was one big one, at least two hundred pounds, who looked as if he could pick up a bus with one hand. The one with the gun acted big but was probably not a leader. There was a taller and older-looking one toward the back of the room who I fingered as the leader. And then there was the quiet one in the corner. He sat with his feet up on a pile of bricks and he had a wooden match in his teeth. His eyes were alert and intelligent, and he was staring at me. The others didn't even seem to know he was there.

Finally the tall one stepped out in front of me. "What do you want?"

"I got something to sell you."

"How do you know I want to buy it?"

"You'll buy it."

"What is it?"

"I know who raided you."

He said something in Chinese and that started a racket in Chinese. Then he said, "OK, who did it?"

I laughed. "Come on. I tell you who did it, then I don't have anything to sell you anymore."

"How much are you selling for?"

"Ten thousand dollars."

"You are not in the position to make deals, mister," the tall one said.

"Like hell I'm not."

He hit me hard across the face with the back of his hand and he hit the sore spot where Lenny had gotten me. "Now you tell me who raided us," he said.

"I'll tell you what I'll do," I said. "I'll tell you what his name is for free. For ten thousand dollars I'll bring him to you. His name is Frank Santucci."

They all looked at each other. They didn't know who he was and that was good. That meant that they still needed me.

"Who is Frank Santucci?" the one with the gun asked.

"He brings drugs to the Lower East Side. You guys were on his turf."

"No," the one with gun said. "Gus Harper runs the Lower East Side. We deal with Gus Harper. He runs the East Side."

"Not anymore, he doesn't. Besides, I'll bet you never met Gus Harper. Who'd you make your deal with?"

"Gus Harper."

"Did you meet him?"

"No."

Then the tall one asked, "And where do we find this Frank Santucci?"

"I told you. I bring him to you for ten thousand dollars."

That set off more Chinese chatter and I resumed my circling. It felt better to be moving. I got to the point in my circle where I was facing the quiet one in the corner. He was still watching me and our eyes met. I stopped walking and we just stared at each other. Slowly he got up and came out into the middle of the room. The talking died down quickly until it was so quiet that I could hear him breathing as he stood less than a foot away from me.

He had delicate features. He had a tight small mouth and a sharp strong chin. His eyes were canyons of hidden thought and they didn't move. I don't think he even blinked. He was going to be either my savior or my executioner.

"What is your name?" he asked. His English was impeccable, and his voice was soft and deep.

"Margolis. Eddie Margolis."

"What kind of name is that?"

"It's a bad one, but it's the only one I got."

"You look like a spic."

"I'm half Cuban. What's your name?"

"King Ti Chiou."

"You look Chinese. Do I call you King or Chiou?"

"Call me King. Tell me, what makes you think we're interested in your information?"

"It's your gang."

"And what is it you think we will do when you bring us this Frank Santucci?"

"That's your business."

"I see. You just want your ten thousand dollars, right?"

"Right."

"You think we will kill him?"

"I told you. That's your business."

"I know what my business is, Eddie Margolis. I want to know what you think my business is."

"I haven't thought about it."

"OK. Let me tell you. We'll kill him."

"So what?"

"You like that?"

His eyes looked through me. There was no hiding anything from him. He was smart. He knew what I was doing, and he was going to show me that he knew. That was all right with me. I could play along. "I have a grudge against him."

"So you bring him to us and we kill him."

"Like I said, so what?"

"You have a tough way of taking out a grudge."

"It's a tough grudge."

"What did he do?"

I pointed to my swollen cheek.

For the first time King smiled. "I see. So you get ten thousand dollars and we kill the guy who busted up your face."

"Exactly."

"You're smart, Eddie Margolis. You're really smart."

"That's funny. Lately people have been telling me that I'm stupid."

"That's because they're too stupid to see how smart you are."

"Not you though, King."

"Now we understand each other, Eddie Margolis. How do we know that you haven't made up this story to get us to take out your grudge for you?"

"You mean how do you know that Frank Santucci is the man you want? That's easy. I'll prove it to you."

"How?"

"He's going to confess."

"How will you make him confess?"

"That's my problem. Your problem is getting up ten thousand dollars."

"No. I haven't got a problem. You've got a problem, because we told you that you are not in a position to make a deal."

"And I said, 'Like hell.' No deal? Fine. I'll go back and finish my dinner." I started for the door. I might have made it if it weren't for the giant's tree trunk of an arm. He grabbed me by the collar and threw me across the room like a Wiffle ball. Someone caught me and landed a couple of punches in my back. I saw them all start to move in around me. It was going to get out of control. I looked over at King and he smiled at me. We understood each other. I was in for a hard time.

Things started to move quickly. The giant took hold of one of my arms. I reached down and grabbed a piece of pipe and took a vicious swing at his head. He turned to avoid it and I got him on the back of his neck. He didn't go down, but he was hurt bad. Then I flew across the room and went for the kid with the gun. I gave him a hard crack on the wrist with the pipe just as he was pulling the gun out of his belt, and I heard the bones break and the gun drop to the floor. Somebody went for it but backed off just in time to miss a kick in the face.

I grabbed the gun and threw my back against the door. "OK! That's enough," I said. I was out of breath, but nobody moved. I had a gun and a pipe and their attention. The giant was rubbing his neck with both hands and eyeing me cautiously. Everyone else waited to see if someone would move against me. But nobody did. King sat calmly on his chair chewing his match stick.

"Listen, fellas, I didn't come in here blind," I said. "That raid has got you guys scrambling. You want to be tough? You want to be back out on the street? Listen to me. You want Frank Santucci and I can bring him to you. You make a deal with me and I'll stick to it. But don't kid yourself, King. I don't need you to do my dirty work. I just thought you guys might want to go along for the ride. You think about it. If you want me, leave word at a bar on Avenue A near Seventh Street called The Pit. I'll make a straight deal. But don't try anything funny. I haven't even started to show you what I can do."

I backed out the door and then bolted. I retraced our route coming up and made it back to the kitchen of the restaurant. I fled through the restaurant, noticing that my table was clear except for a bill and a fortune cookie. I threw a ten-dollar bill down and grabbed the cookie and made for the street.

When I was about ten blocks away I pulled the gun out of my pocket and dumped it in a sewer. Then I slowed down and opened the cookie. My fortune said, "Do not play with tigers unless you are a lion."

Chapter 18

The rain hit before I made it out of Chinatown, and I ducked into one of those tacky gift shops for tourists and bought a brightly painted wooden umbrella for two dollars. I felt a little silly walking up the Bowery with a Chinese novelty item, but the rain was heavy and at least it kept me dry.

The streets were deserted by the time I got up to my neighborhood, but when I was just a few blocks from Houston Street I saw a small figure, about a block away, walking toward me. There was something familiar about the walk, and as I got closer I realized that it was Little Danny.

He didn't have an umbrella and he was drenched from head to foot. His hair clung to the sides of his face and made him seem even smaller than usual. He wasn't wearing his glasses and there was something wrong with him. I knew what it was as soon as I saw his eyes. They were rolling in that wild kind of way that junkies' eyes do when they need a fix. He looked bad. Real bad.

He would have walked right past me if I hadn't grabbed his arm and turned him around. He was shaking uncontrollably.

"Danny, man, what's the matter with you?"

"Eddie, I need money."

"OK, Danny." I reached into my pocket and pulled out a twenty-dollar bill. That was all I had to my name. "Go get fixed, Danny. You look terrible."

"I need more, Eddie."

"That's all I got, Danny."

He grabbed my shirt and pushed me against the building. "I need more!"

I pushed him off me. "That's all I got, Danny."

"I need more! Get me some more, Eddie!"

I got a knot in my stomach. He called me by my name and he knew who I was, but I meant nothing to him. I was just a body that might be able to get him more money, and I wasn't anything else. I'd seen junkies like that before. He'd kill me if he thought it would get him fixed.

"What happened to your supply?" I asked.

"I'm not fucking around! I need more money!"

"It's not like you to get caught short. I'll give you what I got, Danny, but . . . "

He grabbed the umbrella out of my hand and tried to swing it at my head, but it was open and the wind caught it and all he managed to do was bang it against the wall. All of the wood split and suddenly he was holding a handle with little broken strips of painted wood hanging from the end. So much for the two-dollar umbrella.

If I hadn't just had a close call with a bunch of Chinese hoodlums, it might have been comical to watch Little Danny swinging this contraption of broken wood at me. Maybe I was losing my sense of humor. I grabbed what was left of the umbrella and dropped it in the street. Then I took him by his wet collar and threw him up against the wall. I threw him hard and it hurt him, not enough to do any damage but enough to straighten him out for a few seconds. I held him there against the wall and then he started to cry.

"Hey, c'mon, Danny. Talk to me. What's your problem? I thought you were too smart to get caught short. Stop crying."

"It's drying up, Eddie," he said through his sobs. "They tripled the prices." He said a lot after that, but I couldn't understand a word of it through his crying. I remembered what Murphy had said about the streets drying up and the junkies going wild. Something was going on. I loosened my grip on him, but I didn't let go.

"Why don't you go to Jack's? Somebody there'll fix you up."

He stopped crying, but his voice was still shaky. "They

can't fix me, Eddie. Willis and Curry, they went to Harlem to cop. They don't know what they're doing. Eddie, I don't want to go to Harlem.''

He'd always be the nice Jewish boy from the suburbs. Little Danny had no right being a junkie. I let go of him, and he quickly slipped past me and started down the Bowery.

"Hey, Danny."

He kept walking.

"Hey, Danny!" I ran after him and grabbed his arm. He spun around, only this time he had a knife in his hand.

"Leave me alone, Eddie."

"Give me the knife."

"Leave me the fuck alone." And he took a halfhearted jab at me.

I backed out of the way and put my hands up. "OK, Danny. OK." I started walking backward with my hands in the air until he turned and walked on. He didn't turn around again. I didn't exist anymore. Or so he thought.

I followed him back down the Bowery toward Chinatown. Somewhere on the block ahead of him I saw a head stick out of a doorway and then disappear. I walked fast and held my breath as Little Danny walked past the doorway, but nothing happened. As I approached the doorway I swung away from the building and kept near the street. It was some kind of textile warehouse with a big metal door, but there was nobody there. Maybe I had imagined it.

The rain began to fall even harder as I approached Chinatown for the second time that evening. I thought of buying another two-dollar umbrella, but I was already soaked through to the bone. The wet streets glistened with the reflections of the streetlights and neon signs. The sound of the rain on the parked cars and garbage cans drowned out all the other sounds, except for an occasional swish whenever a car drove by. There were a few Chinese people, dashing from building to building, and a few tourists determined to enjoy their evening out despite the rain.

On a quiet corner just south of Canal Street a white

couple stood under a dark awning, waiting for the rain to
let up. Little Danny stopped in front of them as if he were
going to ask them directions or something, but I saw the
knife come out. I bolted toward them and caught up to
them just as Little Danny was grabbing the woman's pocketbook. I came up behind Little Danny and the couple saw
me. Their reaction made Little Danny turn around, but I
was ready for him. I kicked the knife out of his hand, and
when he bent to pick it up he slipped on the wet sidewalk
and went down on his hands and knees. I jumped on top of
him and laid him out flat and pulled the knife away from
his reaching hand. It was an old rusty switchblade with a
point as dull as a butter knife.

The woman picked her pocketbook up out of a puddle
and the man stood over us, not knowing what to do.

"I don't know how to thank you," he said.

"Don't thank me. Just get out of here." I threw the
knife into a pile of garbage in front of a closed-up fruit
stand.

"Don't you think we should call the police?" he said.
He was standing half under the awning and half out in the
rain. He had New Jersey written all over him.

"The police? Are you crazy? Do you know who this
is?"

"Honey, let's get out of here," the woman said.

But the man couldn't resist. "Who is it?"

"This guy belongs to the Terrorists. You know who
they are?"

They both shook their heads.

"Jesus! Take your things and get out of here before the
others catch up to us. I'll take care of this one."

They looked at each other. The woman held her dripping wet pocketbook out in front of her. "Let's go, honey,"
she said. And they left.

Little Danny started to struggle underneath me.

"Don't move, Danny."

"Let me up."

"Listen to me, Danny. I'm going to get you some
drugs."

He stopped moving.

"Now it's going to take a little time. Can you wait an hour?"

"No!" And he started struggling again.

"Danny, listen to me. I'm going to get you drugs. Do you understand me?"

He was crying again. I could tell by the way he was breathing. "C'mon." I stood him up and held his wrists so he couldn't slip away. "Now trust me, Danny. I'm going to get you fixed."

Walking into The Pit was like a trip back in time. It was still early and it was pretty empty, but Leon was at the bar with some of the other regulars and I could almost see myself sitting there with a booze-induced grin and a scotch on the rocks. None of them would have noticed me if Ivan had not made such a fuss over me at the door.

"I don't believe my fucking eyes!" he announced. "It's Eddie goddamned James Bond Margolis himself!"

They fell all over themselves trying to buy me a drink and I finally had to pull Abraham down to the other side of the bar to get two coffees. Ivan put his arm around me while Abraham made the coffee.

"Damn, Eddie, for someone who doesn't drink anymore, you sure are wet!"

Everyone laughed.

Leon broke away from the group and came down next to me and Ivan. "Hey, Eddie. Isn't that Little Danny from Jack's?"

Little Danny was sitting by himself at a table in the back. He looked pitiful.

"Yeah, that's him."

Leon's face got serious. "Eddie." He couldn't get himself to say what was on his mind. "Eddie."

I knew what was coming and I smiled at him. "What, Leon?"

"Eddie. You're not . . . Eddie, you're not banging up, are you?"

"No, Leon. I'm not banging up."

His face relaxed. "You had me worried there for a minute, Eddie. You stop drinking and then you show up here with a junkie. Hey, Eddie, he don't look so good."

"Yeah. He don't feel so good, either."

Leon laughed in spite of himself. Then he got serious again. "Hey, Eddie. You know who was in here the other day, looking for you?"

"Gloria."

"That's right. I guess she found you. I didn't think you'd mind me telling her where you live, the way she looked and all."

Abraham set down two mugs of coffee in front of me. "We been hearing some shit 'bout you, Eddie," he said.

"Yeah? Don't believe a word of it."

"I'm serious, brother. You fuckin' wit' some bad people, man. You hear me?"

"Hey, Eddie can handle himself," Leon said. "Can't you, Eddie?"

"I've been doing all right up to now."

"Yeah, well, you watch your Cuban ass, brother."

"What are you worried about, Abe? I don't owe you any money."

That sent Leon and Ivan into a rampage, and I left them laughing and brought a cup of coffee over to Little Danny. I told him to sit tight and then I went to the telephone. Dropping the change into the phone, it occurred to me that this was the same phone I had used to call the cops after I had found Tony. I wondered for a moment where I would have been now if I hadn't made that call. But I didn't have to wonder too long. There was an empty stool next to Leon.

I called Nadine Wolfe.

"Wolfe residence," someone answered. I recognized the voice.

"Pierre?"

"Yes?"

"This is Eddie Margolis. You hit me on the head with a wrench. Remember?"

"Oh, sure. How are you, Mr. Margolis?"

"Pierre. I have to talk to Nadine. It's important."

"I'm sorry. She's not here, Mr. Margolis."

"Where is she?"

"She's out at the Hamptons."

"Can you give me the number?"

"I'm sorry, Mr. Margolis, but I'm not allowed to."

"Pierre, listen to me. I'm going to give you a number where I am. I'm in a phone booth. Call Nadine and ask her to call me. OK?"

"I don't know if I'll be able to reach her."

"Try. If you can't reach her, call me back."

"OK, sir."

I gave him the number and then hung up. I sipped my coffee and waited, but I didn't have to wait long. The phone rang about a minute later.

"Well, you see, Eddie. I knew I'd hear from you, but I didn't think it would be so soon." Nadine's voice was light and happy.

"Nadine, I have to talk to your husband."

I could hear her breathing on the other end of the phone. "Nadine?"

"Eddie, I told you. My husband died three years ago."

"Nadine, I have no time for games. Are you out at his place now?"

"Eddie, I don't know what you're talking about. I'm at Gus's. Well, actually it's mine. I just bought it from Gus today. He's left the country."

"Where'd he go?"

"I don't know."

"C'mon, Nadine. I have no time for this. I know all about you and Gus. I know who Gus is. Now I'm not going to tell anyone, but I have to talk to him."

"He's in Brazil."

"Call him."

"What for?"

"I need some drugs. Not for me, but for some friends of mine. The whole city is drying up and I've got to get my hands on some drugs quick. I don't have any money. Your husband is the only one who can help me."

There was silence on the other end of the phone. I looked down at the puddle that was forming on the floor from my wet clothes. I watched Leon showing off how he could drink a shot of scotch without using his hands. And I checked on Little Danny shivering in the corner. It didn't look as if he were drinking his coffee.

"Eddie?"

"Yeah."

"This is a favor, Eddie."

"I know."

"You may have to make it up to me one day."

"OK."

"I'll try to reach him, but he may not be in yet. I have the number, but you can't always get through. Stay there and I'll have him call you."

"OK. Make it fast. Things are bad down here."

We hung up. This time it was a long wait. I called Gloria and told her that I was trying to help Little Danny and that I'd be over as soon as I could. Then I sat with Leon and had another cup of coffee. I was trying to comfort Little Danny and I was working on my third cup when the phone rang.

I reached it after the second ring. "Hello?"

Somebody said something in Spanish, but it didn't sound like a call from Brazil. It sounded like a wrong number from the Bronx. Then I heard my name. We spoke in Spanish.

"Who is this?" I asked.

"Is this Eddie Margolis?"

"Yes."

"The man call me. He say I give something to you. You come and get, OK?"

"Sure, where are you?"

"Never mind me. You see Mario."

"Who's Mario?"

"Fifth Street. B and C."

"Where?"

"You find him, man. He at the store. He hold for you." And he hung up.

Little Danny was standing in front of me shaking like a belly dancer. I smiled at him. "OK, Danny. I got it. Let's go."

We walked back out into the pouring rain and I started across Avenue A, but Little Danny held me back. He had calmed down a little. I guess knowing that it was coming was helping.

"Where are we going, Eddie?"

"See some guy named Mario on Fifth Street." I tried to walk, but he held me.

"Where on Fifth Street?"

"I don't know. At a store between B and C. What's the matter, Danny?"

"Eddie, we can't go there?"

"What do you mean?"

"It's bad there, Eddie."

"It's bad everywhere, Danny. C'mon." I dashed across the street and he followed, but he stopped me again at the corner.

"I don't have any money, Eddie."

"That's all right. You don't need it."

"Jack got jumped there."

"Danny! For Christ's sake, what's the matter with you? You want drugs or don't you?"

"Let's get Jack."

"What for?"

"Please, Eddie."

We stood there in the pouring rain. Something was very wrong. Here I was offering a strung-out junkie free drugs and all of a sudden he was being picky about the neighborhood. Maybe he knew something that I didn't know. Maybe it really was a war zone down there. Maybe I should have left him and gone to Gloria's. But he wasn't going to last much longer.

"OK," I said. "We'll go get Jack."

Chapter 19

Things were bad at Jack's. Willis was rolling around on one of the mattresses with a pillow over his head. His hands were ripping the pillow apart and the stuffing was pouring out all over the mattress and the floor.

Jack was in his chair, but he was rocking back and forth and his face was all scraped up. There was dried blood around his eyes and his cheeks. He was in the middle of a screaming match with Curry who was dancing in circles around the chair. Little Danny and I sneaked in unnoticed.

"Jack, I can get drugs," I said.

Jack kept screaming at Curry.

"I can get drugs!" I screamed.

That worked. Not only did I get Jack's attention, but I got everyone else's too.

"You don't need money. Just sit tight for a few minutes and I'll bring you drugs."

"Shit, where you gonna get drugs from?" Curry asked.

"I got somebody over on Fifth Street ready to hand it over to me. I just got to walk up there and pick it up. Give me ten minutes."

"Fifth Street! Shit!" Curry turned his back and walked into the far corner.

"You can't go to Fifth Street, Eddie," Jack said. "I just came from there and look what they did to me. It's a riot up there."

"It's always a riot up there. What's the matter with you guys?"

"Eddie, I'm telling you." Jack was keeping his calm. "They'll jump you going in because they think you got

166

dough. Or the cops'll grab you because they think you got dope. Or the junkies'll grab you on the way out and get your dope. There must be a thousand of them up there. And cops, Eddie. Fucking cops on horses. Believe me, Eddie. You can't get to Fifth Street.''

"Jack, in another couple of hours you guys are going to be in serious trouble. Now I got a guy on Fifth Street waiting to hand me a bag. Free! I don't care if you get it or not. I'll go home. That's where I was going when I ran into Little Danny. But you get me to a guy named Mario on Fifth Street and I'll get you dope. Think about it.''

"Mario?" Curry's voice came from the darkness. "Ain't that the guy from the store up there?"

"Yeah," I said. "They told me to see Mario at the store.''

"How you gettin' it, Eddie?" Jack asked.

"Never mind that. Can you get me to Mario?"

"Curry, ain't that the guy you used to work for?" Jack asked.

Curry came out of the corner and stood behind Jack's chair. "Yeah, that's the guy from the store.''

"Can you get me to him?"

"You can go by Sixth Street," Curry said. "But Sixth Street ain't no better than Fifth Street. They got stores over there too.''

"What about from B?" Jack asked.

"Shit, man. You got to walk through half a block of buildings.''

"C'mon, Curry," Jack said. "They must have a route.''

Curry didn't say anything. I could see him trying to get his drug-deprived brain to function.

"What's a route?" I asked.

"It's an escape path," Jack explained. "All the stores have them, so if the cops come in you got a way out through the buildings. They can't follow you and you come out a block away from the store. They never get you.''

"I can do it!" Curry said. He was grinning from ear to ear. "I can fucking do it! Ed-dee! I can do it!"

I had to smile. It was so easy to make a junkie happy. "Good, let's go."

"Eddie, you sure you can get it?" Jack asked.

"I'm sure."

"Good, I'm going with you."

"Me too," Little Danny said.

"No, Danny," Jack said. "You stay here and keep an eye on Willis and these guys." He pointed to the mattresses. "We'll be back in fifteen minutes. Tops."

"Jack, I'm scared. What if . . ."

"No ifs, man!" Curry said. "I can fucking do it! Ed-dee!"

It was still pouring when we stepped outside. I saw a head disappear into the doorway of a building across the street and it was not my imagination. I wanted to see if I were being followed, but I knew that I had to get Jack and Curry to Fifth Street. Whoever it was would have to wait.

Avenue B near Houston Street was in that place somewhere between order and chaos where you can still recognize enough of the world to think that maybe nothing is wrong. Cars still drove up and down the avenue splashing the sidewalks with water. Thin dark men hung out under the awnings of the groceries and drank beer and smoked cigarettes. There were a lot of police, but most of them just stood around in their big yellow raincoats and swung their nightsticks like batons. Junkies stood in small groups in doorways or out on the corners in the rain. It could have been just another night in Alphabetland.

But it wasn't.

A cluster of police in riot gear stood in a small circle at the intersection of Avenue B and Second Street. They were watching a junkie flap around in the puddles like a fish. They jabbed him with their nightsticks in a disinterested sort of way, and finally two of them picked him up by the arms and legs and carried him off to a paddy wagon parked nearby. The junkie wiggled and squirmed and tried to yell out, but his voice was suddenly drowned out by an uproar from within the paddy wagon. Junkies tried to push their way out of the door when it opened and the cops used the junkie they were carrying to block the exit. They pushed the whole mess of them back inside.

Things got worse. There were junkies everywhere: white junkies, black junkies, Latin junkies, prostitute junkies, punk junkies, hippie junkies. Everywhere I looked there were little scuffles between police and junkies. The police were in full riot gear and they were swinging their clubs, but not like batons. The police would merge on one block and try to round up all the junkies, taking a few with their clubs and losing the rest to the other side of the street. Then they would cross the street and get a few more. The junkies were all being piled into paddy wagons, but it was a slow process.

As long as we stayed away from the waves of police action, we were all right. We tried to walk in the middle of the street and to keep moving, but sometimes we would have to wait in the shadows for the violence to break up. The police were calm and methodical, picking up junkies and dragging them off. They knew time was on their side.

Near Fourth Street we found our way blocked by three big cops with rifles. Curry and Jack fell in behind me, and I put on a big smile and raised my hands. "We're just trying to get out of here," I said.

The cops didn't move.

"Tell us which is the best way to go, we'll go," I said.

One of the cops looked behind him and then came up and grabbed my arm. "Go up Fourth Street to Avenue A and get lost. And I ain't telling you you won't get clobbered on the way."

They let us pass. We made as if we were going to turn up Fourth Street and by the time we got there the three cops had disappeared into the confusion. We kept walking.

Fifth Street was completely blocked off. A line of cops on horses two-deep stood at the intersection. The cops had rifles in their hands and their helmets were pulled down to cover their faces. Beyond them was a full-scale riot. The air stank of tear gas, rendered useless in the rain, and the street was filled with bodies and broken glass.

Curry stopped in the middle of the intersection, twenty

feet from the line of cops, and stared under the horses'
legs down Fifth Street. Jack tried to pull him, but he
wouldn't move. Finally, with my help, we got him to start
walking, but he'd lost his cool. "Jesus Christ! Did you see
that, Jack?" he asked.

"I saw it, man. Keep moving, Curry. You got to show
us where to get in."

When we got through the intersection, Curry stopped
again and put his hands to his face. I tried to pull him
along, but Jack stopped me. He stood in front of Curry and
held him by his arms.

Suddenly I was hit from behind and I went down on the
wet street. I saw Jack and Curry take off and then felt the
stampede of junkies falling all over each other, trying to
get away from a line of cops on horses. The cops were on
top of us, and one of them leaned over on his horse and
took a swing at me. I saw an opening in the line and I
somersaulted through, missing the club and ending up
behind the line of horses. The cop who had swung at me
turned around to find me, but I was up and running. He
pulled his horse back into the line to get the junkies who
couldn't run.

I caught up with Jack and Curry in a doorway on the
west side of Avenue B. Without a word Curry bolted
across the street, stepping over bodies left in the wave of
attack, and slipped through an open window of an abandoned building. I looked at Jack to see if Curry knew what
he was doing, but Jack took off the same way Curry had. I
counted to three and then followed.

Once I got through the window the drop was longer than
I had expected, and I landed on my hands and knees in
total blackness. I stood up and said, "Now what?" more
to make sure that Jack and Curry were there than anything
else.

"Wait for your eyes," Curry said.

We stood perfectly still. All we could hear from outside
was the rain and the clop of horses' hooves on wet pavement. With one quick jump we were miles away, but we

were nowhere. I reached my arm out and felt a wall. It
was wet and clammy.

"OK," Curry said. "Let's go."

"I can't see anything," I said.

"Hold on to me."

"Is Jack here?"

"I'm here, man."

I reached out in the darkness and found a warm wet
shirt. "Is that you, Curry?"

"Hold on," he said.

I felt Jack grab my shirt and suddenly we were walking
through total darkness. After about three steps I tripped
over some large immovable object and I had to hold on to
Curry to keep from falling.

"Slide your feet," Curry said—the junkies leading the
blind.

And we kept walking through a vacuum of darkness,
sliding our feet across a floor we couldn't see. I lost track
of time and space. It seemed like fifteen minutes before we
hit a wall, but it was probably more like thirty seconds. I
held Curry with one hand and felt the wall with the other
as we inched our way along. There was a dull knocking
sound, and I stopped and held Curry back.

"What's that?"

"It's my foot, man. I'm looking for the hole."

We moved slowly, listening to the rhythmic tapping of
Curry's foot against the wall. And then he missed a beat. I
felt his body crouch down and then come back up.

"OK. This is it," he said. "Let's just hope it ain't
guarded."

I followed Curry through the hole. It was a crawl space
about two feet by two feet that went through the wall. I
had to get down on my stomach and wiggle through. It
would have been all right if it weren't for the rats. I
couldn't see them, but I felt them running over my head
and my back. I crawled faster and I heard Jack cursing
behind me.

The hole emptied out into a room lit by a candle that sat
on a cinder block in the middle. We dusted ourselves off

and blinked in the brightness. The walls were painted in blotches of pink and green, and you could make out old pieces of ripped-up furniture and cabinets still hanging from the walls. This had been somebody's kitchen.

From there it was easier. Curry took the candle and we walked through room after room, building after building. Each time we entered a room we could see the rats scurry into the corners and disappear behind piles of broken wood and beer cans. In one building a rotten stench filled my nostrils and it grew worse as we went on. We had to hold our noses so that we wouldn't vomit. I kept my eyes on Curry's back, not wanting to see the cause of the stench.

Finally we came to a room with another candle. There was a door that was obviously of more recent construction than the rest of the building. It had a skull and crossbones drawn on it.

Curry knocked hard.

The door opened and a face appeared. "What you want?"

"Mario," Curry said.

"No Mario here," and the face disappeared. I heard a body slam against the door, but Curry must have put something there to keep it from closing.

The face came out again. "No Mario here, babe . . ."

Curry shoved his weight against the door and it flew open. Jack and I came in behind him.

There were two Puerto Ricans in the room and a lot of candles. There wasn't much else except for the machine guns that they were pointing at us.

The one at the door was smiling. "I do you favor and say no Mario here. You come in anyway. OK, you in."

"Where's Mario?" Curry asked.

"I tell you. No Mario here."

"Tell him Eddie Margolis is here," I said.

"He no would care."

"Try him," Curry said.

"You Eddie Margolis?" the other one asked me.

"Yeah."

"Go see Mario," he said in Spanish to the one at the door.

The one at the door slipped out a window in the back of the room and came back a few seconds later. He said, "OK, you. This way." We started for the window, but the other one stood in our way. "Just Margolis," he said.

I was led out the window onto a fire escape in the back of the building. We climbed up to the next floor and into another room which was well lit by candles all around the edge of the floor. There were three men in combat uniform with machine guns. I felt as if I were in Nicaragua. There was a big old wooden desk in the middle of the room, and behind it was a big Puerto Rican with his feet up on the desk and a lot of jewelry around his wrists and his neck. His armpits were stained with sweat and he wore a headband that was also soaked with sweat. He was drinking Diet Pepsi from a can.

"Who are you?" he asked.

"I'm Eddie Margolis. Who are you?"

"I'm Mario," he said, as if it were obvious. Maybe he thought there was a nameplate on the front of his desk. "Man, somebody been lookin' out for you." He brought his feet down and opened a drawer in his desk. He pulled out a bag of heroin and threw it across the desk at me. There was still a machine gun in my back, so I didn't move.

"Yes, baby, somebody look out for you. The man send me a message. You know what he say? He say the man call him from goddamned Brazil to make sure you get this shit, man. Fucking Brazil, man! Come on, sit down over here, man." He nodded to a chair in front of his desk and I sat in it.

"You want soda?"

No, I didn't want soda.

"Carlos, get him a soda. I tell you what, baby." He put his feet back up on the desk. "I supposed to give you three bags. Usually, I don't know. Maybe they go for one each. No, I guess one and a half each. So three bags, that means four and a half thou. Today, you see what happens today. What did you do? Did you come through the route?"

Somebody handed me a Diet Pepsi. As I reached for it I

felt the point of the gun in my neck. "Yeah, I came through the route. Hey, tell him to take the gun off me."

Mario waved him off and the guy stepped back and let the gun fall to his side, but he was watching me. I opened my Diet Pepsi. Nothing ever tasted so good.

"You never worked here," Mario said. "How did you know the route? Well, never mind that. OK, baby, so what I'm saying, you get four and a half worth of goods, right? Never mind the three bags, you get four and a half thou. Well, OK, baby. I'll tell you what I do. OK. I give you five. You like that, man? You get five. 'Cause I tell you what. You see it out there. One bag gets you five, easy. The man tell me I can sell for what I can get. We sell nickels for fifty. I tell you, a bag can get you five. So I give you one bag. For you, because the man call from Brazil and he don't know there's a fucking war going on here. Go ahead. Take it."

I leaned forward and grabbed the bag.

"Is the route the only way out of here?"

He laughed. "Oh, baby, you something. You want the free bag and a way out too? There ain't no way out, baby. That's why that bag'll get you five. In half a hour the cops be all over this place, man, like you wouldn't believe. I was you? I'd get my ass outta here."

I took a couple of gulps off my Diet Pepsi. "How come it's drying up?"

"How come? Mario don't know how come. Mario sits here and gets rich. The longer he waits, the richer he gets, the more he's gonna get his ass fucked over. It's a game, man. If I'd left a hour ago, I'd be safe now, but I'd be ten thou poorer. You got me? How come it dries up? Nobody tells Mario nothing. The man say sell what you got and get what you can and get out. That's what the man say. You ask Mario why is it drying up? I tell you what I think. I think they gonna sell."

"Sell what?"

"The buildings, man. Clear out the dope and the junkies and sell the buildings so some rich dude gonna make a lot of bucks. That's what Mario thinks. There's only one business in this city makes more'n drugs and that's the real estate, baby.''

I thanked Mario for the bag and the soda, and I was led back outside and downstairs. Jack and Curry watched me nervously, and I smiled and nodded to them. It was as if I had given them permission to breathe. We left the candles and the machine guns and heard the skull and crossbones slam behind us.

"C'mon, let's see what you got!" Curry said.

I pulled the bag out of my pocket and showed it to them. Who the hell needed three bags? This was enough to have my ass thrown in the slammer for ten years.

"Holy shit, Ed-dee!" Curry was literally jumping up and down. Then he came to take it out of my hand. I held it tightly and shook his hand loose. Then I shoved it back in my pocket.

"What's this, Eddie?" Jack asked. It wasn't a friendly question.

"Not until we get back," I said.

"Oh, fuck that, man!" Curry said. "Give it to me!" He moved closer to me. I didn't like this at all. I jumped back from them and picked up a piece of two-by-four from the floor. I held it up like a baseball bat, ready to swing.

"You want it now, Curry? You'll have to kill me. You guys got to get me out of here first."

"Eddie, don't fuck with us, man," Jack said.

"Look, Jack. Mario says that in thirty minutes this place is going to be crawling with cops. I'm not going to sit here with two stoned junkies and wait for them."

"I kept my part of the deal, Eddie," Curry said.

"Not yet you haven't. You got to get us out of here."

Curry started looking around for a weapon.

"C'mon, Jack," I said. "Back me up. You know if you guys do it now we'll never get out of here. Wait ten minutes and you can do it in your own apartment. No cops. No Mario. No nobody. C'mon, Jack."

Jack ran his hand through his wet hair. He was a desperate junkie, but he was also an experienced one. He was convinced already, but he knew he would have a hard time convincing Curry.

Curry picked up a long piece of wood with a couple of nails in it. "Give it up, Eddie."

Jack stepped between us. "He's right, Curry. We can wait ten minutes."

Curry didn't move. He was probably sizing us up, wondering if when it came down to it Jack would take my side or his. We stood like that for a while. Curry wasn't going to give in, and the longer we waited the closer Jack got to going back to Curry's side. I had to take a chance.

I dropped my wood and pulled the bag out of my pocket and threw it to Curry. He dropped his weapon and caught the bag with a surprised look on his face. Already we were friends again.

"Do what you want, Curry. Me and Jack are getting out of here."

I picked up the candle and started to walk. I took a few steps and turned. Curry was holding the bag. Jack grabbed it out of his hands.

"I'll hold it, man," Jack said. "Let's go."

Chapter 20

Avenue B had not gotten any better when we climbed out of the window with the dope in our pockets. Two junkies were on us with knives before Jack was even all the way out. They must have seen the gleam in Curry's eyes. They stood with their knives out, not saying anything. They would wait for us to decide whether we wanted to fight or give up. There were three of us and two of them, and I had no doubt that we could take them, knives or no knives, but I also had no doubt that the cops would be on us in a matter of seconds.

Jack pulled the bag out of his pocket and for a brief instant I thought I was going to see the unthinkable. Then I watched as he carefully ripped off a corner of the bag and handed it to them. If the bag was worth five thousand dollars, then what Jack was handing them was worth at least a couple of hundred, and they took it and ran. Junkies are only greedy up to a point.

We started our slow and careful journey downtown through the masses of police and sick junkies. Curry walked quickly and we had to keep slowing him down so that he wouldn't draw attention to us.

We were down by Second Street and I thought we had made it out when suddenly Jack took hold of my arm. "Eddie, we're being followed."

"Probably just a couple of junkies," Curry said.

"No, man. These ain't no junkies. Don't turn around." And he kept walking.

I thought about the head I had seen on the Bowery and again across the street from Jack's. "Yeah, he's been following me for a while," I said.

"You seen him?" Jack asked.

"Yeah, I've seen his head, ducking into doorways."

"This is somebody else then. It's a car. Don't turn around. The lights are off and it's creeping along the curb about a block behind us."

"What makes you think it's following us?" Curry asked.

"One of these days, Eddie, you gonna tell me what kind of shit you in," Jack said.

Jack pulled the bag out of his pocket and ripped off another corner. He put the corner back in his pocket and then he slipped the bag to Curry. It was well done. It looked as if they were shaking hands. "Curry, man. Go back to my place and see that they all get fixed. Don't show them the bag or you'll be dishing out to every junkie in town. Just get them fixed. Remember, don't show 'em the bag. I'm gonna take Eddie for a run down Second Street so we can lose this cocksucker in the car. Walk slow, Curry. Remember. Walk fucking slow."

We split up at the corner, Curry continuing down Avenue B and Jack and I turning across Second Street toward Avenue C. Second Street was pretty empty. When we were about two thirds down the block I casually glanced back toward Avenue B. There was a big white car parked down near the corner that hadn't been there before. On another street, in another part of town, I might not have noticed it. But here it was as obvious as a white politician in Harlem.

When we turned the corner onto Avenue C, Jack ducked into a stairway that led down toward a basement apartment. Our eyes were at street level and from the quiet darkness of the stairwell I watched the car take the turn onto Avenue C with its lights out. It stopped at the corner directly in front of us. The car had New Jersey plates.

Jack was jiggling the door behind us. It seemed to be making a lot of noise and it wasn't opening. I heard him swear. He swore to himself, to me and to Jesus Christ. Then suddenly he stopped and I heard him sigh. He whispered to me, "I got the wrong goddamned building."

It was too late to move. The door on the passenger's

side of the car opened, and a big man in a raincoat stepped out and stood with one foot still in the car. He put up a big black umbrella and looked up and down the street. Then he stuck his head back in the car and said something to the driver. His voice was drowned out by the rain. He stepped all the way out of the car and slammed the door, and the car took off slowly down Avenue C.

The man walked slowly across the street, coming toward us. It was Lenny, Mr. Outboard-Motor Oil. He held the umbrella with one hand and had the other in his raincoat pocket. He moved closer to the building and then he was staring right at us.

His face lit up with a smile and he pulled his hand out of his pocket, gun and all. "There you are, you little misguided shits. For a minute there I thought you'd actually thrown a loop on me. C'mon up, Margolis. Let's see what you got."

He whistled and waved the car back, openly showing the gun in his hand. Jack and I climbed up the stairs with our hands in the air.

"I understand you don't like to hear 'good-bye' for an answer," Lenny said. "You been sticking your face where it don't belong again. Well, now we got something for you."

Then I saw the foot.

It was an ordinary foot, wearing an ordinary sneaker, but it was at least six feet in the air and it was coming down on the back of Lenny's head. The first sound we heard was a dull thud when it hit Lenny's head, followed by the clank of the gun dropping and the casual slop of the body collapsing in a puddle on the street. And then the body that the foot belonged to landed gracefully over the collapsed body. It was King.

The car began a quick trip in reverse down the street toward us and Jack took the lead back around the corner of Second Street. King and I followed, and all three of us got caught in the headlights of another car driving toward us at an unfriendly speed. We made a bolt for a wire chain-link fence and then through an empty lot. As we ran I heard the cars skid to a halt behind us and the slamming of car doors. We were jumping over a brick wall at the back of the empty lot when the guns started. Jack led us over another fence, and we made a dash through the rubble of bricks and mortar of a torn-down building and then over a wooden fence into another empty lot.

From there Jack led us through alleys and courtyards and then across Third Street into an empty building. We climbed through the building and out the back and then into another building that faced Fourth Street. We stopped in the basement of this building, and Jack led us to a group of old mattresses thrown on the floor and we all collapsed to catch our breath.

Suddenly the room became illuminated with the light of a match and Jack lit a candle that sat in the middle on the floor. It was a big room and the front part where we sat had been partially cleared out. The mattresses were propped up against the walls and there were old wooden boxes in the corners like coffee tables.

"This is my hideout," Jack explained, pulling his kit from his pocket and laying it out on the floor. "I fucked up, Eddie. I pulled us into the wrong stairwell. I thought we'd be able to sneak back here, but it's been so long that I forgot which building it was. You remember that guy Trap, started freaking out a few years back?" He pulled the dope out of his pocket. "Yeah, well, the cops were after him and we hid him out here for about a week. Then one day he got restless and they got him. You remember that, Eddie? Hey, who's this guy?"

"King," King answered. "Who are you?"

"Name's Jack. You got one hell of a kick there, King."

"Who are the guys with the guns?" King asked.

Jack already had a belt around his arm and held one end of it in his mouth. Through clenched teeth he said, "I don't know, ask Eddie."

"You're a junkie," King said.

"That's observant, King." Jack held a spoonful of drugs over the candle. It had been a long time since I'd been this close to someone shooting up and I felt sick. I started to talk just so I wouldn't think about it.

"The guys out there work for Frank Santucci. The guy you kicked is named Lenny. He's the one who busted up my face. I didn't see the other guys, but I'm sure they're all together. They're probably after me because I sneaked in and talked to the old man, Frank's father. Frank's the man you want, King. He's also the one who killed Tony."

"Who's Tony?"

"He was a friend of ours."

Jack was filling up his needle from the spoon.

"Why do you do that?" King asked.

"Don't start with me, man," Jack said.

"I'm not starting with you. I just don't understand."

"You want to understand?"

"Yeah."

"You want to understand?"

"Yeah!"

Jack held the needle up in the air, filled with smack. "You know what they call this, man?"

"What?"

"Liquid sky." He pulled the belt tight around his arm and moved his wrist up and down until the veins were popping out. "Liquid fucking sky," he said and he jabbed the needle into his arm.

"I still don't understand," King said.

Jack slowly slipped the dope into his veins and then pulled the needle out and loosened the belt. "Try some, man. Maybe you will."

"Do you shoot up, Eddie?"

"No."

"You deal?"

"No."

"How'd you get mixed up in this?"

"Let me tell you something about Eddie, man." Jack was going into a slow nod. "I been around for a long time, man. I seen some shit. Eddie understands this, don't you, Eddie? He's not as far away from it as you think. You still drink, Eddie? He knows what I'm talking about. He's been there, man. When there just ain't nothing else to do. If you had the guts, maybe you'd kill yourself. But most people aren't that strong. So you do it the slow way until it becomes what you are. And the only thing that makes it better is doing it more. Until you forget why you're doing it at all.''

I watched the shadows from the candle flickering on the walls and ceiling. Maybe I did know what Jack was talking about or maybe it was just stoned-out junkie babble. I had not thought about drinking all day. Let's see, it had been just a little over a week now. A week and two days. It had gotten easier. Today had been easy. But that's because I had been running around all day. Now I could have used a drink, but I didn't really need one. Someone once told me that when he quit smoking cigarettes he didn't start again until he felt like he wanted one but didn't need one. That's the hard part, I guess. It's easy to fight it off when you need it, but not so easy when it's just a question of wanting it.

"Liquid fucking sky," Jack said and he laughed to himself. "I been off it a few times, man. Did you know that, Eddie?"

"I've heard it said."

"It's the fucking truth, man. Twice, man, I've been off it. You know where it got me? Nowhere. I was nowhere, man. Lost in the sauce. You don't understand that, King, but Eddie does. Hey, that was one hell of a kick, though, I'll say that. You know why you don't understand nothing, King?"

"No, tell me."

" 'Cause you're looking for something."

"What am I looking for?"

"See, man? See what I'm talking about? It doesn't fucking matter what you're looking for, man. Maybe you'll find it and maybe you won't. It doesn't fucking matter, man, because you . . . you'll start looking for something else. Let me tell you something, man. Whatever it is you're looking for, it ain't there. And if it is there, it ain't what you think it is. Oh, man, you don't understand shit.''

"Tell me what you want about yourself, Jack, but don't tell me about me, because you don't know me. You don't know where I'm from.''

"China. Big fucking deal."

"I'm from Hong Kong, but that's not what I'm talking about. You're spilled. Spilled? How do you say that word? I can never say it right. Spoy-illed?"

"Spoiled?" I asked.

"Yeah, that's it. Spoiled. You're spoiled, Jack, and you're lazy, that's what you are. Yeah, I'm looking for something. Something maybe you don't want. But that's your problem, not mine. You know why I left Hong Kong? I killed a man, Jack. With my bare hands I killed a man. I was fourteen years old and I killed him for ten dollars. You just put ten times that much in your body for kicks. Don't tell me I don't understand anything."

"You don't understand shit."

King got up and stood in front of Jack. He was mad, but it was his own fault. Nobody should listen to a junkie who just shot himself full of junk.

"Sit down, King," I said. "He's higher than a kite."

"You smashed Vernon's wrist, Eddie, and I didn't get mad at you. You had to do it. But this one. He sits here with a needle sticking out of his arm and he thinks he knows everything."

"Sit down, King."

"Somebody should ship him to Hong Kong. Then let him tell me I don't understand anything."

"You're wasting your time, King. He's wasted."

King sat down next to me. "You have some wild friends, Eddie."

"Yeah, well, so do you."

"How come you asked us for ten thousand dollars? You don't really want any money, do you?"

"No. I just wanted to sound realistic. People don't trust you unless you're being greedy."

"How are you going to get Frank Santucci?"

"I'm going to get him to confess."

"To what?"

"What he did to you guys."

"And your friend?"

"If he did it."

"Now you're not so sure."

"I'm not sure about anything."

"And if he confesses? Then what?"

"I don't know. Turn him in, I guess."

"Turn him in? To whom?"

"The police. You guys. Whoever wants him."

"What guys?"

"The Black Tigers."

"Hah!" King stood up again and began pacing around the room. "There are no Black Tigers."

"Yeah? Then who were all your playmates?"

"What you saw, Eddie, was just a scared little bunch of Chinese immigrants who didn't know what they were doing. You saw them, Eddie."

"They were pretty pathetic," I had to admit.

King stopped in front of the candle and stared down at it. "The Black Tigers was a new gang. My brother was the leader. He was the one with the connections up top and back home and the guts to break in here. He knew what he was doing. He was killed with the rest of them in the raid. There're a few of us left, but that raid took the wind out of us. We couldn't hit back now even if we knew who to hit."

"Hey, Eddie, man." It was Jack.

"What, Jack?"

"Those guys are still out there."

"How do you know?"

"They're looking for you, man."

"I know."

"You watch yourself, Eddie. They're looking for you."

"OK, Jack."

King stood over the candle and stared into the flame.

"And so what do you get out of this, King?"

He laughed. It was the first time I'd heard him laugh. It was a very American laugh. "I want to get the guy who killed my brother."

"Get him how?"

He laughed again. "Eddie, you keep hoping that I'll kill him. Well, I keep hoping that you'll kill him. Both of us want him dead, but neither of us wants the blood on our hands. I killed a man once, Eddie. Once is enough. I'm starting college in a few weeks. I busted my ass for that. I practice my English every day. Nobody's going to take that away from me, Eddie. Not you, not the police and not Frank Santucci.''

"Your English is very good."

He squatted down in front of the candle and smiled. "Thank you, Eddie. I pride myself on my English. It's my way of proving to myself that I can adapt to anything. Not like your friend here. Eddie, do you have a plan to get Frank Santucci, or are you just running around and making trouble?''

"I'm running around and making trouble. I haven't got a plan. But I have got an idea.''

"What is it?"

"We've got to get out of here first."

"I think we should stay here for the night. Jack's right about one thing. Those guys are still out there and they want you, Eddie.'' He blew out the candle.

I lay in the darkness and listened to the sounds of King and Jack breathing. The mattress was as comfortable as a cement floor. I couldn't sleep. I wished that I could tell Gloria where I was. I missed her.

Chapter 21

The morning sun had already dried the sides of the burned-out buildings on Fourth Street and had left only a few puddles scattered in the potholes of the street and the cracks of the sidewalks. The buildings were three-story brick tenements with cinder blocks in the doors and plywood in the windows. New red and white posters were pasted to the cinder blocks in each doorway and stuck out from the dried dirt and graffiti-covered walls with a certain eerie consistency. I stuck my head out the window and strained my neck to look at the doorway of the building that I was in, and I could just make out the red and white of the poster on the grimy facade.

Jack was in the middle of the street now. He looked carefully around him and then looked at me and gave a comical shrug. He walked back to the building that we had spent the night in and when he was close enough to speak in a normal tone of voice he said, "I don't know, Eddie. It's pretty fucking quiet. I don't see nobody. No men in white cars, no junkies, no cops. Nobody."

"Maybe it's all over," I suggested.

"Could be. It's hard to believe."

"Jack, can you get me one of those posters?"

"Which posters?"

"See those red and white ones? All the way up the block?"

"Yeah."

"They're on each door."

"So?"

"Get me one of them."

He climbed the steps of our building and ripped the poster down. I got off the crate I was standing on to make room for him and in a few seconds his feet slipped in through the window.

The poster was made of heavy cardboard and was about the size of a normal piece of paper. The word NOTICE was printed across the top in bold red letters. Underneath, in slightly smaller black letters, it read, THIS PROPERTY SUBJECT OF AUCTION BY THE DEPARTMENT OF HOUSING PRES-ERVATION AND DEVELOPMENT—SEPTEMBER 5, 1986. There was more printed underneath that, but I didn't have to read it.

"What is it?" King asked, trying to read over my shoulder.

"It's an auction. They're selling all of the buildings on the block."

"Yeah, it's more than just this block," Jack said. "I seen those posters all over the place. Up on Fifth Street, Sixth Street and all along the avenues."

"OK," I said. "We got to get out of here."

"Where are we going?" King asked.

"Jack, you go back to your place and get a couple of guys. Nobody too fucked up, OK? Meet me back here in half an hour."

"What are we doing?" Jack asked.

"This is the bait," I said, holding up the poster. "We're going to get Frank Santucci."

"What about me?" King asked.

"I'm going to need you. You come with me. I gotta find a phone."

"Eddie, I hope you know what you're doing," Jack said.

Avenue B looked like a police convention. We had not even turned the corner, but we could see them. Two cops in riot gear pulled their guns and approached us. Yesterday their guns might have seemed big and nasty, but last night I had had machine guns pointed at me and now these looked like water pistols. It was no wonder that the government was losing the drug war.

We all put our hands in the air. "We're not junkies," I said.

"I don't fucking care what you are," the bigger one said. "Put your hands up against the car and spread your legs."

The bigger one kept his gun on us and the other started to give King a patdown. I suddenly realized that Jack was still holding and was going to be in trouble.

"In case you haven't heard," the one holding the gun said, "this area is subject to a twenty-four-hour curfew. Now, what are you guys doing out here?"

The other one finished with King and started on me. "Officer, I need to see Detective Murphy," I said.

"What'd you say?" he asked.

I spoke louder. "I said, I have to see Detective Murphy."

"You mean from narcotics?"

"That's right."

"What'cha wanna see him for?"

"I have some information for him."

The other one finished me and now was working on Jack. Poor Jack.

"Well, why don't you tell it to us, and we'll tell it to Detective Murphy for you."

"No. I have to see Murphy myself."

"Hey wise guy, you don't *have to* do anything except what we fucking tell you. You're out on the street when there's a curfew in effect. You could get six months for that."

The other one had finished giving Jack a patdown without finding anything and I had to smile. Jack had been around long enough to know how to carry without getting caught. Somehow it gave me the confidence to stand my ground.

"Well, what I have to say is for Detective Murphy," I said.

"All right. You want to fucking talk to Murphy, you'll fucking talk to Murphy. OK, Jeff, handcuff them."

We all got a set of handcuffs and they left us by the car. It didn't seem as if there were anybody in particular watching us, but the street was crawling with cops and we'd look a little suspicious, walking around with handcuffs on. Jack winked at me once, but otherwise we just stood there and felt the sun start to get hot. We waited a long time.

I was standing with my handcuffed wrists on top of the car, looking at nothing in particular, when I heard Murphy's voice behind me. "You look good in handcuffs, Margolis." He was standing with a uniformed cop and he was wearing that big smirk on his face.

"I look good in anything," I said.

"Oh, I don't think you'd look so good in the slammer. OK, take the cuffs off this one, would you?" The uniformed cop took the handcuffs off me.

"Let's take a walk, Margolis," Murphy said.

We took a walk right down the middle of Avenue B with nothing around us but cops and cop cars and paddy wagons.

"Looks like you got yourself in some trouble, Margolis. Being caught out in the streets during a twenty-four-hour curfew."

"So what?"

"I don't know. Six months in jail if we really wanted to sock it to you. What are you doing down here?"

"What do you think?"

"I try not to think anymore. I didn't sleep again last night. Must be this goddamned job. I'm a fucking mess, Margolis. Listen, I looked into Gus Harper a little. You might be on to something there. We've been trying to get Mrs. Wolfe for questioning, but we can't find her."

"She's in Southampton."

"With Harper?"

"No. You missed Harper. He's in Brazil."

"What about Santucci?"

"That's what I want to talk to you about. I'm gonna nail him."

"You've said that before, Margolis."

"I need one hour and a deserted street. I need you and a couple of cops, and I need a tape recorder."

He stopped and looked at me. "Anything else?"

"Yeah, I need those two guys back there let off. I need a couple of junkies who live down near Allen Street and I need some rope."

He raised his eyebrows. "Anything else?"

"Yeah, I need a gun." He started to say something, but I cut him off. "No bullets. Just a gun."

"Anything else?"

"No."

He stared at me for a long time. I didn't count the minutes, but it took longer than it should have to decide whether or not to grant my requests. You could have had a midlife crisis in the time it took him to say anything.

He finally let the smirk sneak back on his face. "Margolis, I hope to God you know what you're doing."

Chapter 22

Jack, Little Danny, Curry and Willis watched me wrap the rope around King's body and arms. The only way to make it look 100 percent realistic was to do it right, and it would be better to err on the side of realism. King did not move as I tied the ends of the rope tightly around his wrists. Then Jack and I leaned him over slowly and laid him facedown on the floor.

"How do you feel, King?" Jack asked.

"Like live bait."

"Good, that's what you are," I said. "Got anything to say before we gag you?" I asked.

"Yeah. I hope you know what you're doing."

He turned his head so that we could slip a gag into his mouth and then he lay with his cheek on the floor, staring out into the room. We were in the front room of an old railroad apartment in one of the burned-out buildings on Fifth Street. The apartment was empty. The windows had not been boarded up so there was plenty of light.

Curry pulled his head in from the window. "Eddie, there's a couple of cops coming down."

I stuck my head out the window. It was hard to believe that this was the same street we had seen the night before. Broken glass and bricks were still scattered all over the place, but the street was empty except for Murphy and two uniformed cops coming toward us.

"OK, Danny. Go get them."

"Eddie, man! They're fucking cops!" Willis protested.

"Willis, I told you there'd be cops here and I promised that the only thing that was going to happen to you was that you'd get some free dope. Now don't start with me! Go ahead, Danny. Bring them up here.''

Little Danny hesitated until Jack nodded his approval and then he walked down the hall to the apartment door. We heard him going down the stairs and then we heard nothing.

"Eddie, man," Curry said. "I hope you know what you're doing."

"Relax."

We heard voices downstairs and then the clobber of feet coming up the steps. Murphy came in first, followed by Little Danny and then the two cops. The front room was suddenly crowded with people.

"You got the tape recorder?" I asked.

"Right here." And he lifted it and showed it to me. "Remember, Margolis. It ain't gonna be worth thirty seconds in court if you threaten him."

"Don't worry. He's gonna tell you everything you want to know, all on his very own."

Murphy shook his head. "He ain't gonna talk with all these dope addicts around."

"They won't be here."

"OK, Margolis. Where do you want me?"

We set Murphy and the two cops up in the next room. The room was dark so they could stand in the shadows without being seen from the hallway. We pushed the microphone through the crusty wall so that only a piece of torn-up wallpaper separated it from the front room. We tested it a few times and it picked up everything.

Then we waited.

Frank showed up right on time. He parked his car at the corner as I had told him to and then he walked down the middle of the deserted street. He didn't look so good, but then again, none of us did. Jack and Little Danny slipped into the first room nearest the door and hid in the shadows. I walked Curry and Willis to the door, went over their parts with them again and then stood at the door with the empty gun in my hand.

I listened to Curry and Willis go down the steps. The

fact that you could hear people walk down the steps was
an extra bonus that I hadn't planned. There was a long
period of silence. It seemed as if an hour passed. I switched
the gun to my other hand and wiped the sweat on my
pants. Finally I heard feet coming up the steps. I tried to
figure out how many people there were, but I could only
tell that there were more than one.

The door swung open and Willis came in first, with
Frank immediately behind him. I was almost too surprised
to move, but I pushed the barrel of my gun against Frank's
temple. "Don't move, Frank."

Curry came in behind us and grabbed Frank's arms.
Willis gave him a patdown and took a gun out of his belt
and a flask out of his inside jacket pocket.

"I thought I said no guns, Frank," I said.

He looked at me with his green bloodshot eyes. "I can
be careful, can't I?"

We pushed him down the hallway into the front room.
He didn't even look into the rooms we passed.

"Let me at least have my flask," he said, standing
awkwardly in the middle of the room.

I nodded to Willis and Willis handed him the flask.
Frank took a long pull from it and then offered it around.
There were no takers. His shirt was hanging out from
underneath his sports coat and his hair was uncombed. He
looked like a drunk who had just been dragged into the
precinct.

Curry and Willis stood in the doorway inspecting the
gun. "You need us, Eddie?" Curry asked.

"No, go ahead. I just wanted help getting his gun."

"You want us to wait outside?"

"No. Go home. Frank and I want to talk in private."

"What about my gun?" Frank asked.

"What about it?"

"Shit, Eddie. That's a nice gun. What are a couple of
junkies going to do with it?"

"Anything they like."

"Thanks, Eddie," Curry said, and they left. We listened to their steps on the stairway. A few seconds later

we heard Curry laugh out loud from the street. It had a beautiful effect; for an instant I believed that I was alone with Frank and King. I put the gun in my belt and sat down on the floor with my back against the wall about ten feet from Murphy's microphone. Frank walked slowly around the room and then stopped in front of King, apparently seeing him for the first time.

"Who's this?"

"His name is King. He killed your brother."

Frank paced around some more and finally sat down, leaning against the wall opposite me, and took another slug from his flask. "Son of a bitch, Eddie. So you got the guy who killed my brother." He couldn't have sounded less enthusiastic.

"That's him."

"What makes you think . . . How do you know he did it?"

"I figured it out."

"You figured it out, huh?" He took another swig from his flask and screwed the top back on and slipped it into his pocket. We were just two men talking in an empty room with a Chinese coffee table.

"You want to hear it?"

He grunted.

"I'll take that as a yes. Charles Wolfe was your financier. He'd been out of the banking business for a long time and he was loaded. He was perfect for the job, except that his past caught up to him. He didn't want to go to jail, so he rigged his death by driving his car off a cliff. He even made it look like his wife was with him. He did a good job, because it worked. Perfectly. But Nadine was too dumb to run the business by herself, so Wolfe came back as Gus Harper.

"Wait a minute, wait a minute." He held up his hand. "I don't want to talk about Charles Wolfe. Tell me how you figured out that this guy killed Tony."

"I'll get to that. Hear me out. Everything was fine, until you figured out a way to make some real money. Drugs are all very lucrative, but it's a lot of work and it's dangerous. You figured out a way to make enough money in one shot so that you could get out of the drug business altogether. But there was one problem. Harper was too powerful. He was more than just a financier. He was running the whole show. So first you had to gain some control.''

I paused to see if he was ready to talk, but he said nothing. I continued.

''You got The Merk under your wing and you used Tony as an intermediary, and that's how you found out about these guys.'' I nodded toward King. ''They were your big competitors when it came to supplying Gus with the goods. But you took care of that. In a big way.''

Frank pulled out his flask, but he didn't open it. He held it on his lap. ''So far I haven't heard anything new.''

''No, there's nothing new there. I just want to make sure that I figured it all out right.''

''You're doing fine, but you're boring me.''

''Well, here's where it gets interesting. Once you knocked out the Chinese, everything was easy. You had plenty of time before the auction to set everything up.''

''What auction?''

''This one.'' And I pulled the poster out of my pocket and threw it across the floor at him.

It didn't reach him and he didn't try to get it. ''How'd you find out about that?'' he asked.

''It's posted on every goddamned building in the neighborhood.''

For the first time his eyes seemed to focus on me. I kept at it. ''It's great to buy property cheap from the city, but it's even better to get it for nothing. I was down here last night, Frank. Your boys can attest to that.''

''Yeah, somebody gave Lenny a concussion.''

''I saw the streets last night. I haven't seen the papers yet today, but I can imagine them. Nobody in their right mind would buy property down here now.''

He was smiling.

''And on the fifth the city will show up with all the deeds and a hammer, and the auction will start. And nobody'll be there. Well, one person will be there. I don't know who it is, but I guess it doesn't matter. Whoever it is will buy four square blocks for cheap, real cheap. What do you think he'll have to pay? For four square blocks in Manhattan? You think he'll pay ten million?''

"Hah! Ten million? Are you crazy? He'll get it for five hundred thousand dollars. Easy.''

"That's wishful thinking.''

"Wishful thinking? You don't understand the real estate market. Everybody says it's location, location and location. Well, they're all fucking wrong. It ain't location. It's timing. After last night this building we're sitting in isn't worth the paper the deed's written on.''

"Maybe, but the city isn't just going to let it go for nothing.''

"You don't understand what I'm saying. Sure, we'll get it cheaper now than we would have a month ago. Maybe we will save ten million or so. But it doesn't matter. If we flooded the streets with dope again tomorrow, the value would go back up, but so what? That's only the icing on the cake. Did you see the streets *today*? OK, last night was bad, but what about today? Do you have any idea what this property would be worth if there were no drugs down here at all? If there were no junkies, no stores, no dealers? If the streets were clean and safe?''

"It's still a shitty neighborhood.''

"That's because you have no imagination. Do you realize that we are in fifteen minutes walking distance from Wall Street? Fifteen minutes. I walked it myself. Three minutes by cab. And let me tell you something else. If you had a building here over five stories tall, you could look clear across the river to Brooklyn, clear downtown to Wall Street and clear up to the Empire State Building. You're talking luxury condominiums worth close to a million bucks apiece. You know what that adds up to?''

"Enlighten me.''

"One hundred million dollars.''

"And the drugs?''

"What drugs? There won't be any drugs. If there's no

drugs, there's no junkies. They'll go to Harlem or wherever they have to go. I'll be sitting on a hundred million fucking dollars."

"That sounds like a lot of money for property in Alphabetland."

"I already have a contract! All I got to do is get the property and clear out the drugs. Then I take what I bought for nothing and flip it for a hundred million dollars. Not bad for a month's work."

"A hundred million, huh? You must have people you have to pay off."

He opened his flask and took a long drink. Then he started to laugh. "Margolis, you're pretty smart."

"How's that?"

"You don't give two shits who killed Tony, do you?"

I smiled at him. It was a smile that I didn't have to fake. He had the bait in his mouth and he was running. "No, not really."

He was still laughing. "Why'd you bring this guy here then?" He nodded toward King.

I shrugged. "I had to have an excuse to get to talk to you."

He took another drink and then slipped the flask back in his pocket. "You're a smart kid, Margolis. I'll give you that."

"How smart?"

"How'd you like to work for me? I could use someone like you. Half the guys who work for me are idiots."

"I don't want to work for you, Frank."

"Come on, Margolis. Besides, I can't do business with strangers."

"I don't want to work for you, Frank. Let's cut a deal and leave it at that."

"No deal. You gotta work for me. C'mon. I'll pay you more money than you'll know how to spend."

I pulled the gun out of my belt and waved it around. "You're not in the position to bargain with me, Frank."

He laughed. He might have been drunk, but he still had

a bellyful of guts. "What are you going to do? Shoot me?"

"Maybe. Or maybe I'll turn you in."

Again he laughed. "Turn me in? Are you kidding? Who's gonna believe this cockamamie story? They'll laugh it right out of court."

"I want ten million, Frank."

"Ten million? Are you crazy? You know how many people I have to pay off? You know what I got to lay out for this thing? I'll give you a hundred thousand dollars. Take it or leave it."

I put the gun back in my belt and pretended to think. "OK. One million bucks. But I want a one-shot deal. I'm not gonna work for you, Frank."

"Why don't you want to work for me?"

" 'Cause I don't want to be around when the shit hits the fan."

"No shit's gonna hit the fan. I'll give you five hundred thousand dollars and you can do whatever you want."

I stood up and paced back and forth as if I were contemplating the offer. Then I stopped in front of him and extended my hand "You've got a deal." He grabbed my hand and we shook. A handshake never felt so good.

"Now what about this guy?" he asked, nodding toward King.

I turned around and looked at King as if I had forgotten him. "Oh, yeah." I walked over to King and casually pulled out the gun. "Should I kill him?"

If Frank was shocked by my casualness, he didn't let on. "You sure you got the right guy?"

"It makes sense, doesn't it? Tony led you guys to the Black Tigers. This guy's brother got killed in the raid. He wasn't going to take on the whole family, but he'd get the poor junkie who couldn't defend himself."

Frank shrugged. "Do what you want."

I put the gun toward King's head and looked at Frank. His face was expressionless. He'd let me do it, but I wasn't going to make it that easy for him. I stood up and held the gun out to Frank. "Here, I'll let you do the honors."

He didn't reach for it. "No, go ahead, Eddie."

"C'mon, Frank. After all, it was your brother."

He hesitated and then took the gun. Then he walked over to King and pointed the gun at his head. I felt sick. For an instant I thought he was actually going to pull the trigger. But he dropped the gun on the floor and, without saying a word, went over to the window and looked out onto the empty street.

I tried to sound impatient. "C'mon, Frank, what's the matter?"

He spun around. Maybe his face was paler. Maybe his eyes were more bloodshot. Somehow he looked even worse than he had when he came in. "You got your story wrong, Eddie."

"I did?"

"This guy didn't kill Tony."

"Oh." I leaned against the doorway with my hands in my pockets. The gun was on the floor between us, but I didn't look at it. "What about the auction and the money?"

"No, that's all right. We still have a deal. You'll get what you came for. You got everything right but for this guy."

I shrugged. "What's wrong with this guy?"

"Nothing's wrong with him, Eddie. It's just that he didn't kill Tony."

I waited a few extra seconds just for the hell of it. Then I said, "Who did?"

And then he got a funny look in his green bloodshot eyes. It wasn't the look I had expected from somebody about to confess the truth. He stared at me and said, "I did it."

I didn't move. I wasn't supposed to care, but I felt the ground give way beneath me. I heard myself say, "Well, what do we do with this guy?"

"Let him go, I guess."

If I had just left it there, just turned and walked away, I might have saved myself from the ugly truth. But I wasn't

satisfied. Everyone had wanted me to get Frank Santucci:
Gus Harper, Gloria, King, Murphy, even the old man. I
needed to know that I had gotten him for myself. So I
pushed just a little bit further and asked the question that I
shouldn't have asked.

"Why'd you kill him, Frank?"

He had his answer all ready.

"Tony was fine working with The Merk. Infiltrating
Harper's camp—no problem. But then he found out about
the real estate angle and got a bad case of morals. Inno-
cent people getting thrown out of their homes, wrecking
the neighborhood so yuppies could move in and on and on.
Suddenly my fucking junkie brother is out to save the
whole world, mostly his fucking junkie friends. He was
going to blow the whistle on the whole fucking thing."
Frank picked up the gun from the floor and slid it in his
belt. "I know what you're thinking, Eddie. I mean, killing
my own brother. But I couldn't let some junkie stand
between me and a hundred million bucks."

"Well, I guess it had to be done," I said, and I turned
my back on him and headed down the hallway. I didn't
take more than three steps before I heard the clicking of
the empty gun.

Chapter 23

I sat on the front stoop of the empty building with King, Jack and Little Danny, and watched Fifth Street fill up with police cars. They handcuffed Frank in the backseat of a patrol car and let him sit there by himself. Cops love to put people in the back of their cars and make them wait. It gives them a good feeling to have a criminal waiting to be driven off to prison. It's like the feeling a teenager gets from a full tank of gas and a six-pack of beer. Murphy was explaining what had happened to Sid Philips. I saw him pointing to the building and to Frank in the back of the patrol car. He pulled out the tape and showed it to Philips. It was already in a little plastic bag and I watched Philips take the bag.

Then a limousine pulled up among the police cars and stopped in the middle of the street, between where we were sitting and where Murphy and Philips were standing.

"Who the fuck is that?" Jack asked.

Philips bent down to talk through the window on the other side of the limousine. We couldn't see who he was talking to, but I saw the tape come out of the plastic bag and go through the window.

"He's givin' him the fucking tape!" Jack said, but I was already up and headed for the limousine.

Philips saw me coming across the street and he yelled out at me, "Margolis, this is police business! You keep out of this!" He started to come around the limousine toward me, but he was too late. I yanked the back door open and looked in. Nadine was there by herself, smiling and wearing a bright pink dress with her bare legs crossed casually beneath her.

"Hi, Eddie."

Philips was around now and he grabbed me by my arm. "Let's go, Margolis. Get out of here." He tried pulling me away, but I stood there, holding on to the open door of the limousine. "Margolis, this is police business, now get out of here before I have you arrested."

I looked over the top of the limousine and saw Murphy watching me. His face was bright red with anger, but he spoke softly. He said, "Get the tape back."

Then from within the car, Nadine said, "Come on, Eddie, all the hot air's getting in. Either get in or get out."

Philips let go of me and I slipped into the limousine next to Nadine. She leaned across me and pulled the door shut behind me. The air stunk of perfume that might have been expensive but wasn't supposed to be used by the gallon.

"I underestimated you, Eddie."

"Maybe you overestimated yourself. What are you doing here?"

"I came to get this." And she held up the tape.

"What are you going to do with it?"

"I don't know yet."

"Nadine, I hate to disappoint you, but that tape isn't worth much. There were seven people in there who heard every word he said. Tape or no tape, they've got him."

"Got who?"

"Frank."

"Frank? I don't give a shit about Frank. It's Charles and me I'm worried about. What's on there about us?"

"What does it matter? He's out of the country, isn't he?"

She pulled the tape out and stuck it into a tape deck built into the console in the middle of the car. She hit the play button and we listened to it. It had come out pretty good. It got everything right up to the clicking of the empty gun.

When it was finished she rewound it. "The fuck I'm too dumb to run the business," she said. "If I'm so dumb, how come I have all this fucking money, and if you're so smart, how come you're so fucking unemployed?''

"Nadine, let me have the tape."

"Fuck off." Then she started the tape again. Every time Charles or she was mentioned, she rewound it and erased their names, so that by the time she was finished Gus Harper was, once again, an unknown. After she had gone through the whole tape she popped it out of the tape deck and held it in her hands.

"How'd you find out about this anyway?" I asked. "How did you know to come down here?"

She closed her mouth and puckered her lips as if she were going to keep a secret. She had about as good a chance as a straitjacket had of holding Houdini.

"Sid told me," she said.

"Sid Philips?"

"Frank's not too smart, Eddie. He wanted Charles's power, but he forgot the most important thing. Protection."

I grabbed the tape out of her hands and stuck it in my pocket.

"You can have it," she said. "But you still owe me a favor."

"I got you Frank Santucci. We're even."

"Maybe you're right. But one thing doesn't make sense to me."

"What's that?"

"If Frank killed his brother, then why did he kill The Merk?"

"What do you mean?"

"Frank told Gus that he killed The Merk to avenge his brother's death."

"Maybe he was lying."

"Come on, Eddie. Why would he lie to Gus about it? Besides, why would he admit to it if he didn't do it?"

I had no answer for her, but suddenly something sat like a lead weight in the pit of my stomach.

Murphy's eyes were sparkling when I stepped out of the car with the tape in my hands. "Good work, Margolis," he said, taking it and putting it back in the plastic bag.

"It's not all there," I said. "I had to give up Charles Wolfe. It's the only way we could get the tape."

He nodded sadly. "Well, we got Santucci," he said.

"Yeah, we got Santucci."

"The tape probably wouldn't have been any good against Harper anyway. Don't be so glum. We got Santucci."

"Yeah, we got Santucci."

"Margolis, he would have killed you. He was trying to shoot you when you turned your back on him. Did you know that?"

"Yeah."

"Well, what's the matter?"

I had a desire to smile and pretend that it was all over, but I couldn't. I said, "We need to make one more stop."

"What for?"

"You probably should bring a couple of men with you."

He stared at me. "Where are we going?" he asked.

"Carmine Street."

Chapter 24

She had the same puffy eyes and the same puckered lips, but her hair was uncombed and matted, and her face was filled with tension. She led me into her dark and smoky living room filled with overstuffed ashtrays and wrinkled-up tissues. The coffee table displayed a stack of dirty dishes and a half-eaten sandwich from Blimpie's. The television emitted a hazy streak of blue light across the room, but the sound of country music was coming from a radio in the bedroom.

She sat down on the couch between a dozen magazines and an empty bottle of vodka. "I was worried about you, Eddie. I tried to wait up, but I fell asleep."

I cleared a couple of record albums off a chair and sat down.

"This mess is all from last night, can you believe it? I had it all clean for you."

"I'm sorry," I said. "Some of Frank's men were following me and I had to spend the night hiding from them. It wasn't safe to come here. A lot's happened, Gloria."

"What's happened?"

"We've got to get out of here. We have a lot to talk about, but there'll be plenty of time on the plane."

"What plane?"

"Pack some things and let's go. We've got to move."

"Eddie, what happened?"

"They got Frank."

She sat up slowly and lit a cigarette. "They got Frank?"

"He told us everything, Gloria."

"What did he say?"

"He told us everything. About the Chinese, about Gus Harper and about the auction."

"He told you about the auction?"

"You knew about that, didn't you?"

She nodded and inhaled on her cigarette. "What did he say about Tony?"

"He said he killed Tony to keep him quiet."

"He . . . did he . . ."

"No. He didn't mention your name at all. He took the full blame for Tony and he said it was only because of the money. But we have to get out of here before the cops figure out that he's lying."

She stomped her cigarette out in an empty coffee cup and blinked her eyes. "What do you mean, Eddie?"

"You know what I mean. Now let's go."

"You know then?"

"Yeah, I know."

"How did you know Frank was lying?"

"I found out Frank killed The Merk to avenge Tony's death. He must have done that before you told him that you did it."

She got up off the couch and slowly walked over to me. Then she slid into the chair with me, put her arms around me and started to cry. I held her. She felt warm, she smelled sweet. I probably could have persuaded myself to let her go. I felt her tears on my neck and they tickled as they ran down to the collar of my shirt. But it was too late now.

"Eddie?"

"What."

"Oh, Eddie, don't hate me. I had to do it. Tony was just being crazy. He was so jealous about me and Frank that he was going to blow the whole thing. And Frank would have let him. I worked so hard for Frank and for the auction, for all that money. And Tony was going to blow it because of something we had two years ago. It wasn't fair, Eddie. I couldn't let him do that. Do you understand that?"

"Frank said Tony was against it because of what it would do to the neighborhood and his friends."

"Oh, I don't know. Maybe that was part of it."

"And what happened when you told Frank that you were the one who killed Tony?"

"When I first told him after the funeral, he didn't believe it. But then he realized that I was telling the truth and he freaked out. I didn't know he loved Tony so much. And then he told me that he wouldn't see me anymore, and all I could think was that he loved Tony more than he loved me." She broke down into sobs, and I sat still and waited for her to continue.

"And why did you come to me and tell me that Frank killed Tony?"

"I needed something," she said, sniffling and hiccuping. "All those years with him and all of a sudden he was treating me like dirt. I couldn't believe that love could just disappear like that, Eddie. I just couldn't believe it."

"So you told me that he did it so that I would set him up?"

"Oh, Eddie, I know it sounds horrible." She was crying and it was hard to make out what she was saying. "But I was so mad at him for just shutting me out like that. You can't blame me for that, Eddie. One day I was his princess and the next day I was dirt."

She cried in my arms some more, and then she got up and walked to the bathroom and I walked to the window. Out on the street Murphy was leaning against the car, waiting for us, with the two uniformed men sitting in the backseat. I heard the toilet flush and the running of water, and when she came out she looked much better and she was brushing her hair.

"Where are we going to go?" she asked.

"I don't know. First plane to anywhere."

"You think they'll figure out that he's lying?"

"I don't know. But I don't think you want to stick around to find out."

"Do you think he'll go to jail?"

"I don't know. Look, we've got to get out of here fast."

She went into the bedroom and I heard the radio go off.

She came out with a completely packed overnight bag, and she held it up and giggled. "I packed last night. I was going to leave, but I'm glad I waited for you."

I couldn't take it anymore. "Come on, let's go."

"Eddie?"

"What?"

"Do you love me?"

And suddenly it became very hard to breathe. The apartment was smoky and there was no ventilation. It was just plain stuffy. Here was a woman I could actually love. And what was I doing? I was turning her in to the cops. OK. So maybe I was heartless.

When too much time had passed without me saying anything she held me tightly and started to cry again. "I feel so bad, Eddie."

Then she spun around and picked up her bag. Her eyes were twinkling and I couldn't stand to look at her. I turned and opened the door and led her out of the apartment and down the stairs to the street.

Maybe I seemed too eager, or maybe I pulled her just a little too hard. Whatever it was, she stopped four steps from the lobby and froze.

"C'mon," I said, and tried to pull her.

"Eddie, I . . . forgot my cigarettes. I . . . I'll be right back." She climbed back up the stairs and I heard her key in the door. I didn't hear it close behind her.

I waited a few minutes, and then the lobby door burst open and the two uniformed cops came in. "What apartment?" one of them asked me, but the other was already past me and running up the stairs.

"What's going on?"

They didn't stop to answer. I started to walk up the stairs after them. There was nothing I could do now. They'd get her.

Murphy came in the lobby door and held it open. "C'mon, Margolis. You can see from the street."

"See what?"

"Don't worry. They'll get her. She climbed out the fire escape."

I couldn't decide whether to go up or down. Murphy
didn't pressure me. He just held the door open and waited
"She gave you the slip, Margolis."

I came down the stairs and walked past him into the
street. After the darkness of Gloria's apartment and the
hallway I had to squint in the bright sunlight. It wasn't
even noon yet and it was hotter than hell. Maybe we were
in for another heat spell. I followed Murphy out to the car
across the street, and we leaned our backs against it and
stared up at Gloria's building. The two cops were on the
fire escape, just outside her window, and they were climbing the ladder toward the roof. Murphy nudged me and
pointed to the roof of a building about three buildings
away. Gloria was walking quickly, without looking back.
Her bag was over her shoulder. She looked as if she might
have been trying to make a train.

She must have heard the cops as they hit the roof
because she turned and saw them. And then she started to
run. There was a row of buildings with roofs all the same
height. Then there were two that were about one story
higher, and she jumped and climbed up onto the higher
level. The cops were about four buildings behind her.

She crossed the two buildings on the higher level and
then she came to a space between her and the next building. It was about the width of a driveway.

"They've got her," Murphy said.

"No, she's going to jump," I said.

"She'll never make it."

"Yes, she will."

"I don't think so."

She looked back over her shoulder. The cops were
scrambling up onto the higher roof one building away.
One of them had his gun out and we heard him yell for her
to stop. She didn't move, but she didn't put her hands up
either. She took one last look at the cops and then took a
running jump over the open space.

The last thing we saw were her arms reaching for the
building on the other side. She wasn't even close. She
didn't make any noise going down. One of the cops ran

over and looked, and then quickly turned away. The other didn't even look.

Murphy moved away from the car and looked down at his feet. "I'm sorry, Margolis."

I felt a sudden stinging in the back of my eyes. "Yeah, me too."

"I think maybe you oughta get out of town for a while, until this Santucci thing blows over. You know what I mean?"

"Yeah."

"You got someplace to go?"

"Yeah." I started to walk away. I didn't know which way I was going. I just didn't feel like being around cops.

Murphy caught up to me. "You did all right, Margolis. There was nothing else you could've done. You know that, don't you?"

"Yeah, I guess so." I didn't mind him, just then, but I didn't feel like talking.

"Check in with me before you leave though. I'll be down at the station all afternoon. You'll check in with me, right?"

"OK."

The Village was hot and crowded. I tried to focus my eyes on something specific, but it was like being in a dream. I thought about the dream I had of the disappearing roads in the grassy jungle. I thought about King and his perfect English. I thought about Mario and his Diet Pepsi. I thought about anything I could, to stop thinking about Gloria. It was a game I knew I would have to play for a long time.

When I got a few blocks from Carmine Street I heard the sirens, and two police cars passed me. I realized that I was walking home.

Epilogue

Holly gave me five hundred dollars, which she still had left over, and I went to Florida to visit my father in his new trailer on Big Pine Key. The trailer was smaller than the one in Homestead, but it was on the water and he could keep his twenty-four-foot Aquasport right out in front. There was only one bedroom so I slept on the porch where I could watch the moon come up over the bay and listen to the splashing of the tarpon jumping in the canal. In the mornings the sun would wake me up and I would lie perfectly still and watch the herons and egrets feeding in the canal until the sounds of my father or Mary Lou moving around inside the trailer scared them away.

I had never known my father to have a girl friend and the presence of Mary Lou could have been awkward or embarrassing, but she was too much at ease with herself and with my father to let that happen. When they picked me up at the airport in Key West she took my hand and, in her deep southern drawl, said, "Well, so this is Eddie. Sweet Jesus, Mart. From the way you talk about him I thought he was gonna be some kind of Cuban terrorist or something."

My father smiled proudly, though whether he was proud of me or her, I'll never know. He said, "I never said he was a terrorist. I said he was a bum." And then he grabbed me and hugged me and whispered, "It's good to see you, son."

On the first night we all sat out on the porch and watched a thunderstorm come at us from across the bay. The rain was falling gently and the wind was starting to pick up. The leaves of the palm trees scraped tentatively across the tin awnings of the trailer and off in the distance we could hear the rumble of the thunder. The lightning highlighted the bay and the islands beyond it in frequent flashes of yellow and white. With complete accuracy and detail I told them about my adventures in New York. The only thing I left out was what I had felt for Gloria. I wasn't ready to talk about that.

They listened quietly. My father asked a few questions, and every now and then Mary Lou would interrupt with a "Sweet Jesus" or a "Good Lord." For some reason I kept my eyes glued in the direction of a large palm tree that hung out over the canal. With each flash of lightning I could see the large palms leaves twisting gracefully in the wind, and then the whole tree would disappear back into the darkness of the storm.

When I finished we sat and listened to the rain and the wind and the thunder.

"Jesus, Eddie," Mary Lou said at last. "You sure do take yourself some chances, don't you? Reckon you'all got some braggin' material there, Mart?"

"Brag, my ass," my father said. "What'm I gonna say? My son's been sticking his face where it don't belong? That guy really had only one ear, huh?"

"Yup."

"Musta been ugly. Hey, Eddie?"

He rarely called me by my name, and from the tone of his voice I could feel the imminent delivery of one of his sickeningly deadly accurate perceptions. But a loud crack of thunder interrupted him, and when the thunder stopped he was up and going back into the trailer. "Honey, we got any of those fried shrimp you made for dinner left over?"

"Reckon we do."

"Think I could have a snack?"

"Reckon."

I saw him in a flash of lightning holding the screen door open and twisting his head back around toward me. "Come on, son. I want you to try these."

*   *   *

I had been in Florida for almost two months and had an application pending with the Florida Marine Patrol when I got the letter from Murphy. After a week of steady southeast winds the seas were finally calm. My father and I were getting the boat ready to do some fishing out over the reef when Mary Lou came back from the post office with the letter. I sat out on the dock and read it. It was printed on expensive-looking stationery from the Charles Murphy Detective Agency, Inc.

Dear Eddie,

As you will notice from this lovely stationery, I am no longer an employee of the city of New York. I can't tell you how good it feels to say that.

After your departure I made a lot of noise about Philips and Harper, and I talked to a lot of people, including someone from the mayor's office. Nobody listened to me, and all I got out of it was a nice big demotion and a transfer to Queens. It was the nicest thing they could have done. because I quit on the spot and have been happy ever since. The drugs are back downtown, as you would guess, but it's not Santucci or Gus Harper anymore. Who knows who it is? It's not my headache.

Anyway, things are going much better than I could have hoped. Within a week of opening shop here I got two big jobs from an old friend of mine who works for an insurance company. Things went well and I pretty much have the company now as a full-time client. That's good and bad. It's good because it keeps the money rolling in, faster than it ever has before. It's bad because I've been forced to turn down a lot of good work from other sources. Hence, the reason for this letter.

Eddie, I want you to consider this a formal offer of employment. I have seen your work, and I know that with proper training and supervision you could be a first-rate detective. I mean that. You have the right instincts and you're smart, and in spite of everything

I've ever said about you, I don't really think you're lazy. I think you'll work.

I want you to think about this carefully. I don't want you coming back to New York expecting life in the fast lane. The hours will be rough. When you're a small operation you can't afford to take shifts. If you are trailing someone, you have to stay with them. If you're pounding the pavement, you've got to pound it until it responds. Margolis, I'm talking twelve-, fourteen-sixteen-hour days. I'm talking all-nighters. I want you to understand that. And weekends too. Lots of weekends. It's no picnic.

Your starting pay would be an annual salary of twenty-five thousand dollars, plus all expenses. Believe me, I will be generous with raises and bonuses if it works out.

Eddie, I want you to think seriously about this. I want you to think about it because I need you and I think it would work out well for both of us. But I also want you to be sure you know what you're doing. I can't afford to have you quit on me after a few months. I'll need at least a two-year commitment.

So think about it. Call me if you any have specific questions, or if you just want to talk about it some more. I would appreciate hearing from you within two weeks, because if you're not going to do it, I'll have to start looking for someone else.

How's the fishing?

Best,
Charles

When I finished reading the letter I read it again. Then I showed it to my father. The boat was ready: bait, rods, net, gas, ice. My father stood at the helm and read the letter. When he finished he handed it back to me without saying anything and started the motor. Mary Lou wished us luck and we roared out of the harbor, across the bay and out into the ocean. The fishing was excellent and we stayed out all afternoon. We caught some big grouper and some snapper and a bucketful of yellowtails.

By sunset things had gotten quiet. The sun was a big bright orange ball in the west and the clouds all around the horizon were puffy flotillas of pink and orange. It was time to start heading back, but we waited. It's always hard to go back. There's always that one more fish you can catch. The sky was pink, the water was pink and blue, and there was a warm breeze coming up from the Caribbean. Everything was beautiful.

And then I heard the unmistakable ringing sound of line being pulled off a reel at an uncontrollable rate. I looked up, and my father was holding his rod way up in the air and smiling. There was nothing he could do but listen to the music of the line going out. Whatever it was, it was big.

He played it well. He let it run, and when it stopped running he started hauling it in, pulling in some of the lost line. It took another run, and this time he tightened his drag so that the line went out just a little bit more slowly. He hauled in more line. This went on for a good fifteen minutes. I stood next to him with the gaff in my hands. My eyes searched the water for the first sign of the fish, usually a gray and white flash. But the fish was still deep and the water had grown dark and I couldn't see anything but the line cutting back and forth as the fish took its runs, out and back, left and right. The runs grew shorter and less frequent, and my father started pulling in the line faster than the fish could take it out. We had him.

Then the line cut out once more and I watched its angle against the water as it moved out behind the boat in a new direction. The fish was coming up from the depths, but it didn't want to come near the boat. The line swept out further behind us. We both saw it at the same time.

A red and white buoy of a lobster trap sat about fifty feet off the back of the boat and the line was moving toward it. The line stopped moving and the buoy bobbed slightly as the line hit the rope of the trap. Then the line started going out again and the buoy was pulled completely under the water like a bobber. The line stopped and everything was still. My father stood with his rod bending in the air. I don't think we were even breathing. Suddenly with a huge desperate splash the buoy came flying out of the water, like a person gasping for air, and out of the corner of my eye I saw my father's rod straighten, his loose line flapping in the wind.

My father flopped down on the cushioned seats, exhausted by the tension and the physical exertion of the fight. For some reason I felt myself start to laugh. I tried to hold it back, but I couldn't. My father looked at me curiously and then started laughing with me. We laughed for all of the years we hadn't been together to laugh.

Afterward I sat gasping for air, and I realized that the sun was down and it was starting to get dark. "We should go in," I said when I could breathe again.

He sat up and put his rod away in the rod holder. "You thought you loved that girl Gloria, didn't you?" he asked.

I almost started to laugh again. "You're a son of a bitch, Dad."

"Come on. Your father loses a giant fucking fish around a goddamned lobster trap and all you can do is laugh."

"Yeah, I guess I thought I loved her."

"Nothing I coulda done about that fish."

"There'll be others," I said, and realized as I said it that it was the response he had been looking for. He confirmed this by a hint of a smile. "You and Mary Lou gonna get married?" I asked.

"Hell, no. We're havin' too much fun."

"I'm glad you like her. I'm glad you're having fun."

"You mean you're glad I haven't grown old and lonely."

"Yeah, I'm glad of that."

"Seems to me like you were the one growing old and lonely."

"You'll always be a son of a bitch, Dad. Come on. We should go in," I said, putting the gaff away and walking to the front of the boat to pull up the anchor.

"Think you'll take that job up in New York?" he called up to me.

The bow of the boat dropped down in the water from a big wave and splashed me with a fine spray of warm salt water. In my best imitation of Mary Lou, I said, ''Sweet Jesus, Mart, I reckon I will.''